WITCH MIRROR

THE HAWTHORNE UNIVERSITY WITCH SERIES
BOOK 4

A.L. HAWKE

PHANTOM HEART, LLC

ISBN: 978-1-953919-99-1 (paperback)

ISBN: 978-1-953919-93-9 (hardcover)

ISBN: 978-1-953919-70-0 (ebook)

Library of Congress Control Number: 2024901634

This is a work of fiction. Witchcraft is included to infuse a sense of realism to the novel, but in no way is it supposed to represent actual practicing witchcraft, witches, or the religion of Wicca or Thelema. Any satanic groups portrayed in this series are purely fictional and not intended to represent actual people or organization(s). The book also includes fictitious names, characters, places, and incidents. Any public names are used solely for creative purposes. Any resemblance to actual people, living or dead, or to companies, institutions, or locales is entirely coincidental or accidental.

Line edited by Stephanie Marshall Ward

Proofread by Alexa B., alexabooks.wixsite.com/authors

Cover © 2023 by Brosedesignz

Published by Phantom Heart, LLC

27702 Crown Valley Pkwy D-4, #201

Ladera Ranch, CA 92694, USA

Printed and bound in the United States of America

First printing February, 2024

Learn more about A.L. Hawke at www.alhawke.com

Correspondence: contact@alhawke.com

1

———————

TO MORTIFY

"Introducing *Mrs. Cadence Wallace*."

The whole lecture hall goes crazy with applause. Just as I thought—and feared—there's over three hundred faces in our grand hall staring up at me this morning. I smile at Bryce as I slowly make my way up the steps. He has enjoyed calling me *Mrs.* I mean, it was only last spring that he and I got married. And now, as he hands me the microphone to pin to my collar, he even drawls quietly in my ear, "Reeelaaax, babe. You're going to be great."

"I hate you," I whisper, covering my collar with my palm.

I do kind of hate him, you know. I mean, why do I have to do this? Not every graduate student has to lecture.

I'm surprised to see just how dark it looks as I gaze out at the audience. That's good because I see only rows of heads, no eyes staring back at me. Most of the ceiling lights are shining into my face, making me squint when I look up. I place my small leather briefcase on the podium. Then I straighten my navy blue sports coat, throw my long dark hair back, and arrange Bryce's laptop neatly beside my bag.

It grows quiet. Too quiet. Even with three hundred students

in the audience, nobody's saying a thing—until some idiot shouts out, "Way to go *Mrs.* Wallace!" Could that be my best friend, Madison? Probably.

I gulp. Then I wonder if the whole lecture hall hears my throat.

Bryce is right. Reelaax.

"Guys," I say, taking a deep breath, "this metaphysical history class is so special to me."

My voice echoes in the hall. I squint at the bright lights above me again. Then I pause. I say nothing, looking down—for a little too long.

"*Get on with it,*" a mean kid shouts.

"Everyone, please," Bryce says through another microphone. "This—"

"This class is special because it's like...a memorial, you know. A memorial to Doctor Alondra Johansen. This was the class she created at Hawthorne University, and we lost her amazing lectures when she got sick. It was my favorite lecture, too, just as Dr. Johansen was my favorite teacher. I remember looking forward to it every week and, well, Bryce and I, I mean Dr. Wallace and I, are here to try to bring back some of her magic."

There's applause.

So far so good.

"*Way to go, Cadence!*" cries the same girl again in the audience.

Okay, that's definitely my best friend, Maddie. Yep, she loves me. She's not even a student here anymore, but she said she'd come watch to support me.

I press the button on the laptop, clear my throat, and say, "Lilias Adie." Bryce, who's sitting in the first row, gives a reassuring nod.

But then the screen goes blank.

I press the button again. And again. Nothing.

There's murmuring. Bryce furrows his brow, looking over my shoulder. Cocking my head back, I just see a blank white screen.

"Lilias... Adie," I mumble.

I press the stupid return key harder. But Bryce's computer screen goes completely black.

"Lilias... Adie... was, um... a sixty-year-old woman in Scotland wrongly accused by a neighbor of being a witch."

From the corner of my eye, I catch Bryce leaping up the three steps to the side of the stage. Then he looks over his computer, beside me, shaking his head, but he's really no better at computers than I am. I press the damn button again a few more thousand times. Nothing. Then our IT guy, Jay, a heavyset, gray-haired guy in a T-shirt and jeans, climbs the steps.

"Technical difficulties," Bryce says to the crowd.

Bryce covers the mic on my collar and says in my ear. "Just get on with it without the slides."

Without the slides? Is he crazy? Pictures were Alondra's staple, and I spent more time on finding cool slides than on the actual lecture. Mangled, strangled or drowned bodies with dripping red blood was her thing, and all the kids out there were probably looking forward to something like that appearing on the screen behind me. Not to mention, all my notes are on his laptop. Bryce gestures for me to step away from the podium. I shake my head. He actually wants me to stand alone in front of everybody. He *is* crazy. I like this stupid mahogany podium, shielding me from everyone, just fine.

"Lilias," I mutter, trying to remember anything I wrote. "Lilias Adie. She was sixty. An old woman...particularly for that time period."

Great, there's something a second grader could come up with.

"You know, many of you see caricatures of witches as ugly, like old Mother Shipton." I stare down at the mahogany podium. Then I feel Bryce nudge my hip away from the podium again. *No.* I shake my head. But he nudges again. I permit a single step.

Then I stare down at my black flat-heeled boots.

"What about her?" cries another heckler.

"Actually, it was easy for the justice system to accuse any citizen of evil and working with the devil back then. All it took was a simple accusation. And if you were frail, you couldn't do much about it. Women were targeted, particularly feeble, old ones."

Bryce nods with a smile, even though I said it all way too fast.

His laptop falls off the podium.

"Fuck," I say, looking down at his computer. Of course, my profanity is amplified throughout the hall from my mic, sending the audience rolling with laughter. When Bryce picks up his computer, his screen's cracked and still blank. At this point, all I want to do is rush down the steps, run down the aisle, and get the "*fuck*" out of here.

"Cadence," Bryce snaps in a forced whisper, glancing back at me. "Cadence, come on. Cadence, just keep going with it. It's fine."

No, it isn't fine. I don't even have my notes!

Jay, the IT expert, walks to a wall and hits a light switch. The whole lecture hall lights up and, behold, three hundred eyes are staring at me. I can't say a word. I mean, this is worse than ever. I'm looking out, and I just see a sea of eyes. I already went to the bathroom, like, ten times before the lecture started, due to my nerves. Now I don't even know where I left off in my talk. And I have to pee. Again. Some of the people in the back open the outside doors. Students are leaving.

Dr. Kenosha Trent, a dark-skinned woman wearing a curly black wig and a dark blue blouse, walks up the steps with a big smile. She's a witch. A very powerful one. But she's also the provost of Hawthorne University, and I hate her. She overworks my husband and gets in the way of my studies, even sticking her nose into my coven. Right now, she stands on stage gesturing for me to give her the microphone on my collar. Then, unlike me, she prances to the center of the stage, all confident as hell.

"Dr. Alondra Johansen was a very close friend of mine," Kenosha says, looking down. Unlike me, who looked down to avert my eyes, she's doing it as some kind of memorial. That shuts everyone up. "When Doctor Johansen invited me to work here at the university, I was so honored. I had, of course, known Alondra personally for years. But the honor stemmed from the fact that there never was a lecturer as good as she was. Probably never will be." Then she looks right at me. "Lilias Adie, huh, Cadence? Hmm... Lilias had an interestingly disgraceful memorial when she died. But I'll save that for next time, Ms. Wallace. How about we talk of stakes. Do any of you know why witches were burned alive?"

No one says a thing. But that's good because before she got up on the stage, all of them were laughing at me.

I'm leaning over the podium facing her, my heart is pounding, and I feel a surge of fear in my chest. My hand is flapping by my side. Yeah, I'm that nervous. By now, Bryce has picked up his broken computer, stuffed it in his leather bag, and returned to his seat.

"Anyone?" Kenosha asks, gazing at everyone in the class. "Ms. Wallace? Do you know?"

"Purification, Dr. Trent," I mutter. As probably no one can hear, I stupidly holler, "Purification of sins. Burning was to cleanse heresy from the church. Another reason is the belief that burning the body prevented any postmortem sorcery. But most witches were actually hanged, not burned, Doctor Trent. They were hanged by ropes, *then* burned to cleanse their sins."

"Correct, Ms. Wallace," Kenosha says, "and if our audiovisuals were working, we'd show all of those horrible pictures of burning bodies you showed me—that you prepared for class—particularly the ones burned alive at the stake." People laugh. "Burning has been done in many cultures." She starts prancing thoughtfully around the stage. "In India, it was used by Hindus to remove all traces of those who had passed. It was thought that clothes, or any objects, still contain remnants of the soul. The Atman. The one soul. And so, many mendicants keep only their clothes as possessions so that they can pass on freely upon death. But it was in the sixteenth century, far before poor Lilias Adie, when King Henry VIII, the one with six wives, created the first Witchcraft Act. Then it was James..."

She keeps yapping. I can't care anymore. I mean, I totally fucked up, didn't I? Or did I? It feels like it was out of my control. Whatever the case, Kenosha's saving the day again. That's what she does. If it weren't for my love for my hubby, Bryce, and the small semblance of pride I have left, I'd run down the steps, rush down an aisle, and get the hell out of here. But I don't. I'm supposed to be a respectable graduate student at Hawthorne University now. So, instead, I excruciatingly listen to Doctor Trent perform amazingly better with my stolen lecture. Her unprepared performance is so much more assured and polished than mine, even without all those grisly audiovisuals. And, somehow, I feel like the whole thing is being done to show me up. Kenosha hates me too, you know. She's always showing me up—on campus, in front of my friends, even within my coven.

I've learned to hate her head. Right now, she's wearing a curly black wig, but she's totally bald. It's kind of secretive, like she is. When she's being the prim and proper Doctor Trent, she wears fake hair. Then when she accompanies my friends in our sabbaths, she's wigless Willow, the Wicked Witch of the West. I've learned to despise both. Because both of them are always making it known to all my students and witches that she's far better than I'll ever be.

I look down and see Bryce in the first row. He glances up and, the angel he is, flashes me a rueful grin. He loves me, but I screwed up so bad.

When the dean's done and she gets everyone to applaud her absolutely perfect unprepared lecture, Bryce hops back up the steps, takes her microphone, and announces that it's over.

So does that mean... I can run?

I don't run. Being the respectable new graduate student I'm supposed to be, I slowly make my way through the crowds, down the side aisle and outside the lecture hall, morose as hell. No one says a word. Not even my best friend, Madison. But as Maddie meets up with me by the door, her frown kills me.

2

———

EMERALDS

I'M SLOWLY FORKING THIS POT ROAST THAT MY BEST FRIEND Madison's mom, Aunt Jane, cooked. I mix it with some mashed potatoes and peas. It doesn't taste very good. Jane's a lousy cook, but that's not it. I'm not hungry. The smooth red wine is delicious, though. Aunt Jane might not know how to cook, but she really knows wine. And it's quiet.

It's quiet because of me.

Maddie flashes me a woeful smile. She always can sense my thoughts, even when I don't tell her anything. We're just that in tune with each other— ever since we roomed together in the dorms. My brother Damien, on the other hand, is completely oblivious to what's going on. (He's a brainiac, but absent minded. We love him). Bryce is quiet too. So is Dad. He's just quietly cutting some meat beside Aunt Jane at the head of the table, brushing his hand across his short gray hair, sitting up straight for a moment, but not saying a word.

I suppose this somber atmosphere is better than the last time we were all together. Last Thanksgiving we had the worst family fight of all time. I was about ready to cast a spell on my best friend and strike her down with a bolt of lightning for dating my brother. Well, behold: there's Maddie's sitting across from me right now, lovey-dovey with my brother.

I glance at Bryce. He's gathering all his peas on one side of the plate. He's always arranging his food like that. I love it. It's cute.

Aunt Jane let her blond hair grow out long this year. She's pretty. She usually wears rainbow-colored clothes. Not tonight. Tonight she has on a very formal and lovely auburn dress. And she lost weight. She looks really good—almost suspiciously formal. Why? Is there another man in her life? Probably. You know, she's been married like four times.

"So how did the lecture go, sis?" asks Damie. He runs his fingers along his long light-brown hair, pushing it to the side.

Madison slugs him in the shoulder. "She said it was a total disaster, babe," Maddie says. "God, what's the matter with you? Don't you remember? Let's just not talk about it, 'kay?"

My brother shrugs.

"It all went fine after Kenosha saved the day," I quip.

"Great how you are both teaching the same class again, Katie," Dad says. "You and Bryce are inseparable. You're so lucky to have one another, and lucky that the school lets you work together."

Well, not really *lucky*. It was actually planned by Kenosha, but I'm not about to tell Dad. And leave it to Dad to think up something positive to try to lift my spirits. But he doesn't know the dean wants us to work together in order to corral more students into our coven. He doesn't realize just how deep these witches are into my business at Hawthorne U.

"How did Kenosha save the day?" asks Aunt Jane.

"When we had some technical difficulties," Bryce says before swallowing some meat. "Dr. Trent came up on stage and finished her lecture. But she didn't really save the day, Cadence. Our computer was on the fritz. It broke and none of your slides worked. It wasn't your fault. If the computer hadn't busted, your lecture would have been great."

"It was my fault," I object, shaking my head. "I spent all night gathering pics. Alondra always showed the coolest slides. I didn't want to wing it, like you told me to do, when it broke. You know I hate talking in front of people. I have stage fright. It was an absolute disaster."

Dad grins contritely. Jane frowns.

"It's okay, babe," Maddie says, reaching over the table. "Just don't think about it." Then she turns to Damie and opens her eyes wide, signaling for him to shut his mouth.

"Alondra had difficulties with slides." Bryce forks more meat into his mouth. "She just carried on with her lecture onstage. That's all I was telling you to do."

"Well, I'm not Alondra, 'kay?"

"I know," Bryce says. "I know. No...that's not what I meant, Cadence. It was because Alondra had done the lectures countless times before. This was your first lecture. I didn't expect anything—"

"Everything that happened had nothing to do with my preparation. I was prepared. The dean pompously intervened, like she always does. She overworks you, Bryce, and competes with me. She's a complete and utter bitch."

"Cadence," says Dad, dropping a fork and wagging a finger. "Watch your language at the dinner table."

"Sorry, Dad. She stole my show. Yeah, I don't like her. I've said this again and again to you guys. I think she's a total...mean person, and she's overworking you, Bryce. And then when I don't live up to her expectations, she takes over. I mean, it was like she was there waiting for me to screw up. It's like she was expecting me to fail."

"I think she was there to watch you lecture for the first time," Bryce says, shaking his head. "She told me she was looking forward to seeing you talk."

"Yeah, well—"

"She saved us on Halloween," Damien says.

"Damie, would you just shut it!" Maddie cries, hitting his shoulder again. "What's the matter with you?" Then Madison stares at her mom and my dad.

"Are you angry at me, Cadence?" Bryce asks me, squeezing my hand. "I'm sorry. I blame myself for what happened, not you."

"Yes and...no. Bryce, you know I didn't want to do that lecture. The only reason I did it was because we promised to keep things professional. You asked, so I did it. I'm your teacher assistant. But I have total stage fright."

"Even as your professor," Bryce says, "if you didn't want to do the lecture, you didn't have to. I just was hoping—"

"What?" I snap. "What were you hoping? It was a disaster, 'kay?"

Honestly, I'm getting upset that he keeps talking about it. Maddie's right.

"No fighting like last time, kids," Aunt Jane says with a big grin.

That makes us all smile.

"I know how bright you are," Bryce says. Well, apparently, Bryce still wants to talk about it. "I was hoping you could just show everyone you're as good as Alondra. In fact, I think, better. You know you always were Alondra's top student. I just figured you could teach with me this year."

"How's classes this year, Damien?" asks Dad. He's trying to change the subject. That's a very good idea.

"Hard as always. I'm hating organic chemistry. Physiology is pretty cool. But, you know, all my classes are harder than Cadence and Maddie's were. It's not a liberal arts breeze."

"Says you, *doctor*," replies Maddie.

"Science classes are harder," he adds. "It's just common knowledge."

Maddie puts down a forkful of potatoes and lightly pushes his shoulder, as if to hit him yet again. But this time it's totally playful, with a big smile. Then she gets close and pecks him on the cheek. Ugh. Gross! Yeah, I'm never going to be used to them dating.

"I thought you were going to add Bryce's class?" asks Dad.

"I don't know," Damie says. "It'd be kinda weird with him or Kates grading me. It's really for die-hard history majors. Maybe next year."

"Too hard for you, huh, Damien?" asks Maddie with a big grin.

"Well, you could always get *Kenosha* to grade you," I quip. "She likes to butt into everything else I do."

"You know it was actually Kenosha's idea to have you lecture," interjects Bryce.

"Sure, she probably knew I'd fuck it all up." I put the napkin to my lips, and my black lipstick stains the white cloth. Dark lipstick is the only goth thing Maddie and I are wearing. That and our black nail polish.

"It was Kenosha's idea, Bryce?" asks Aunt Jane. She seems oddly disturbed by that. That's weird. You know, I've never seen her even talk to Kenosha, but she acts like she doesn't like her.

Maddie's mom is really nice, but she's so secretive. And as much as I love her, I hate secrets. Maddie told me Jane once knew Alondra, but, for some odd reason, Jane never talks about Alondra either. That makes me angry. It's this occult secrecy that keeps ruining our lives at Hawthorne.

The food on the table and the walls blurs a little. I rub my eyes. Did I have too much wine? Why is everything blurry? And my head's aching.

I rub my eyes.

~

In darkness, I see a dim vision of my backyard. It's nighttime and witches in white clothes and headdresses are dancing around a bonfire.

"Not of dirt, nor bird, nor fire. Bird isn't your mambo. Neither is fire or water. Yours is snake. Or is all this trouble from that oungan?"

~

When I open my eyes, Bryce is talking to Jane and Dad, but I can't hear him. What the hell? It's like someone turned off all the volume in the room. Is he talking about my botched lecture? Probably. Recounting how I could have continued the talk without slides and not screwed everything up?

Maddie nods, replying to whatever he's talking about. Then she asks him something. But I can't hear her words either.

She frowns at me. Then she turns to Jane and my dad. Damie says something. Aunt Jane laughs. I can't hear their laughter.

Something funny, *Owl-Jay?*

I can't hear anything. Why?

I grip my hands real tight. I'm feeling so angry. Why? What am I so upset about?

I want to get the fuck out of this house. I feel trapped. Just like during my horrible lecture, I want to jump up and run out the door. But this time, I can do it. I can just run out. God, I hate Maddie's house. Dad might be all nice and supportive, but not Aunt Jane. You know, she'll support you and act all sweet, then one day get up and leave you just when you need her the most. That's what she did to me. Remember, Cadence?

Yeah. I remember, Alondra.

I stand up and nod.

Why the fuck would Jane care about Kenosha? She's so weird. Look at her smiling at me. She's always acting nice. It's fake. She doesn't fucking care about me. She'll be your friend and then, when everything turns sour, she runs. She really doesn't care about anybody.

"*Oungan!*" I bark. "*Oungan!*"

My own words ring loudly, hurting my ears. Now I hear everything and it's too loud. But no one's saying anything. They're staring at me. But every turn of their heads or shift of their clothes when they move hurts my ears. The air flowing through the air vents in the house blows hard against my ears.

Bryce gestures for me to sit down.

I shake my head.

Tears start flowing down my face.

"Oungan! Did you know him?" I ask Aunt Jane. "Hmm? Did you?"

"Who, dear?" she asks, opening her eyes wide.

"*Oungan!*" I shout. "*Oungan!*"

"Cadence, won't you sit down?" Bryce asks, touching my arm and furrowing his brow. "What's wrong?"

I yank my arm back.

"Did you know Liam?" I ask, shaking my head. "Huh? Answer the question, Jane. Tell us, for once, what you knew about him. Liam and Alondra. You don't seem to like Kenosha, but you never talk about them. Why? Why not tell us, Owl-Jay?"

"What?" Jane's fair skin turns a shade paler. "What did you just call me?"

"Cadence," says Maddie. "Sit down." She's talking in a forced whisper, but her voice is so loud that I practically have to cover my ears. "What's the matter with you?"

"*Did you know Liam, or not!*" I shout at her mom. "*Tell me!*"

"Yes, I knew Liam," Jane says quietly. "Liam was a good friend of mine in college. Why are you asking that now, Cadence? And how did you know my nickname, Owl-Jay?"

"You mentioned that Liam was a student when you went to Hawthorne University?" my dad asks Jane.

"He was a very good friend of mine, Rick," she says with a nod. But she doesn't turn to Dad—she's staring at me.

"Won't you sit down, Katie?" Bryce asks once more.

"And Allie?" I ask, shaking my head. "Huh? What about Alondra?"

Maddie slams her palm on the table and mouths "*no.*" She shakes her head violently. She told me to never mention Alondra to her mom.

"Fine, if not Allie, tell me more about Lee. What was Liam like?"

"Liam was the nicest man I've ever known," Jane says, furrowing her brow. "He stressed a lot in school..." She smiles at the memory. "But his heart was gold. Like yours, Cadence. Yes, I liked him a lot. He reminds me a little of you. Why are you asking me about him now? And Alondra? Won't you sit down, dear?"

"Would you let Alondra sit here if she came over? Would she even have ever fucking been invited to your house?"

"What?"

Maddie grunts. She's getting pissed. Her countenance has changed from pity to looking as angry as I am, ready for a fresh fight.

"Maddie, do you remember how Alondra looked into that oungan's eyes?" I ask, looking up dreamily. "We saw him in our freshman year. Don't you remember? The two of them loved each other so much. Just like you and I, Bryce. We saw them at the Billington House on Beltane."

"You went to the Billington House during Beltane, Maddie?" Jane asks.

"Uh... Well, Mom..."

Maddie not only told me to never talk about Alondra, she also told me to never tell her mom about that Beltane party. She was forbidden to go. That makes two secrets thrown out into the open. Good. I told you I hate secrets.

"Lee and I loved each other so much," I say. "I think we loved each other more than most couples. It was all kept from us, Maddie. Why? Ask your mom. She knows."

Aunt Jane is staring at me now as if I've completely flipped my lid. So is Dad. So is everybody, actually. Maybe I have. But the room isn't blurry anymore—it's very clear. Because I finally get it. I don't know why I didn't understand before, but I understand now. See, Alondra and Jane were best friends. And that leads to a very important question: How could Maddie and I have struggled through so much shit over the past three years at Hawthorne with her mom not saying a word about Alondra? If she knew Alondra so well, why didn't she warn us about her? That makes Jane's sweet smile seem not so sweet anymore. What kind of a so-called *nice* person would not help us through all the hell that Maddie and I, even Bryce, even my brother, went through? And most absolutely horrible of all, what sort of *nice* mom would sit by while her daughter was raped in a witch ceremony?

Trees sway near the windows, looking ready to topple over. I hear a clang of something rolling outside, probably the pots and plants in the backyard garden, being thrown by a sudden gale. Her backyard is full of greenery, and Aunt Jane has a collection of potted flowers. All those things are probably being thrown over in the wind. Water lashes hard against the windows. It's like there's a sudden hurricane outside. The sky was clear when we came to Flintwood.

But although my rage is growing, I actually feel relieved that I finally understand why I'm so upset. I wasn't mad about my botched lecture. I just simply fucking hate Maddie's mom.

"It's like..." I continue looking up, more fucking tears streaming down my face. "If things had worked out better between Lee and me, all the shit that happened to me in Hawthorne—to you, Damien, Madison, to Bryce, and you, Cadence—"

"Watch your language, Cadence!" Dad says again.

"*Stay the fuck out of this, outsider!*" I cry. Everyone gasps. I look up dreamily, thinking of my oungan again.

I miss you so much, Lee.

"Yes, the two of us were in so much love. I think it's the end of my love that cursed the town. Perhaps, if things had been different for Lee and me, evil would never have come here. If others had shown as much kindness as my warlock did, things would have turned out differently. It wouldn't have been so hard for my witches. But Lee had to leave and abandon me, just like you did, Owl-Jay. He had to fucking turn away from his wife and abandon her, just like you fucking did."

"What's gotten into you, Cadence," says my dad. "I don't want you talking witchcraft, and I really don't appreciate this bad language."

I laugh.

At this point, Jane's lost all color. She's as white as a ghost. Well, guess what? It's confession time, bitch. God... Maybe Madison would never have been sexually assaulted if her mother, Jane, had been there for us? My cheeks are burning. My body's shaking. The lights flicker off and on.

"Mom..." Maddie says with wide eyes, staring at me. "I don't know what the hell's gotten into Cadence, but I think I should go talk to her alone, outside, in the backyard. Katie, why don't you and I—"

All the lights shut off. With the storm raging outside, it's now as dark as night, but we still hear the wind shaking the windows and things crashing into each other outside.

"Remember, *Dad's here,* Cadence," Maddie hints.

The lights flash on.

"*How could you leave me!*"

"What?" asks Jane.

"*You bitch!*"

The lights flicker some more. Jane seems to wince every

time the lights blink on, but, for some reason, I'm planning on doing a helluva lot more to her.

"*Why the fuck did you run from me, Owl-Jay?*"

"*Cadence!*" shouts Dad, jumping up. "*Stop this language!*"

I gulp down the rest of my red wine, laughing, while everybody just stares at me. I'm trying to contain myself, but it's taking all my will to not cast a spell over Jane and hurl her across the table, or hurl my wine glass at her. Some of the red wine spills on the table and on my black dress as I gulp. Like I fucking care. Everybody's just waiting for me to talk. It kinda reminds me of my fucked-up lecture this morning.

And the tears keep streaming down.

"Why'd you leave me, Owl-Jay? I fucking loved you. You were my rock. My stone. You and I were so close. When I was attacked by Kenosha—a woman you hated—you abandoned me. You ran and left me with a man who...who didn't understand. A wonderful man, but he and I were ruined because he didn't know what was happening. You could have helped. You hated Kenosha as much as I did. She tried to rid me of my magic. You think I'd let that happen? It ruined my husband! And then it ruined your daughter, Madison."

"*You ruined them, Allie!*" cries Jane, jumping up. And now she's crying too. "*And you hurt Madison!*"

Bryce stands up, putting his hands up between us. "What's going on here. Cadence—"

"Liam couldn't stop it, Bryce," I say, shaking my head. "He didn't understand. But she did. She ran and abandoned us. Why? Why'd you leave us, Owl-Jay? You said Liam was so sweet. Why didn't you care enough about him to help him when he was possessed? Look what it's done to this vessel!" I pound on my chest. "Tell me now, Jane, why'd you leave? You didn't have the courage to say goodbye. You left me, not even paying your respects at *my goddamn funeral!*"

"Cadence!" cries Bryce. "What's happening to you!"

"Oh, my god!" Maddie says, staring at my face. "Bryce, her eyes have turned green!"

I turn and face Maddie. She and Damie lurch back in their chairs.

"*It's because of you!*" I cry, with an outstretched arm at Maddie. "*It's all your fault! You took your mom away from me!*"

I shake. But not completely in anger. I'm getting scared. The words coming out of my mouth didn't sound like mine. My voice has changed.

"*Oh, my god, get out of her, Allie!*" cries Jane. "*My god, get out of that sweet girl! What are you doing inside Cadence, Alondra!*"

"*I hate you!*" I sneer, whirling back to her. "*It took two years after my death to tell you that!*" Now I recognize the voice. It's Alondra. "It takes this vessel to finally tell you what I've been thinking of you all along. The pain you caused me. You hurt me so much, Jane. You were my best friend. Now, hear it from a heart that..." My voice cracks as I weep. "A heart you broke. You can't imagine what it was like when you ran from us. Liam and I were lost... Every simple invitation, letter, email, you ignored. All I wanted to do was apologize. Even see you before I passed. You wouldn't even give me that!"

"I protected Madison from you, Allie!" cries Jane, shaking her head. "From your backward witchcraft! You had turned bad!"

"Some protection. Look what ended up happening to your daughter at ceremony anyway."

That does it. Jane looks like she's going to tear me apart.

"*Get out!*" Jane shouts. "*Get out of my house!* Even Liam left you over your black magic, Alondra! And look what it's doing to you now! You're inside the sweetest girl I've ever known. Leave her body! By god, leave Cadence alone! Leave her body alone! Maddie told me how much you loved her. If you love Cadence, leave her, Allie! Just leave us all alone!"

"Oh, I'll leave. I'll leave soon enough. Don't worry, selfish woman. But whether you wish to help me or Cadence, you're a part of my coven and you're still a witch. You're a *Hawthorne* witch. Abandon me? Fine. But don't abandon our coven. Don't abandon Madison and Cadence."

And with that, I storm out of the dining room.

"Cadence!" cries Bryce. He rushes over to me by the front door. I stop but keep my back to him.

"Go away, Bryce," I say, looking down. Thank god, it's my voice again.

"Cadence," he says, "what's happening to you?"

"That lecture was so humiliating."

"Babe, I'm so sorry. But...is that Alondra inside you?"

I turn.

"My god, Maddie's right, your eyes are green."

Jane rushes toward me, slicing her arms through the air, crying out: *"Vade retro! Get out of Cadence! Vade retro!"*

I burst out laughing. The front door is thrown open by itself. Then Jane is hurled to the ground by some invisible force.

"Apage Diablo!" Jane cries, propping herself up on her elbow.

"Finally casting spells?" I say sarcastically, in Alondra's voice again. "You wish to cast out a devil from this body? Or maybe you want to cast *Cadence* out of *Cadence*? Perhaps I err in seeking your help, Owl-Jay. Perhaps you're too far removed from the craft to understand. Allow me to explain. I am not possessing Cadence. I *am* Cadence. But I am also A-L-O-N-D-R-A. Behold, *we* are the High Priestesses of Hawthorne."

Jane attempts to speak another incantation, but I don't allow another goddamn word to come from her lips.

"I've left you alone to raise your daughter. I granted you the peace you asked of me, Jane. Now Madison is all grown up. If you care about Cadence enough to finally cast incantations to help her, help the town. Or Cadence, the girl you and I love, will suffer."

And with that I rush through the front door. But before I leave, I cock my head back and say to Jane, "Oh, by the way, I forgive *you*, Jane."

"At least let me drive you home, Cadence!" cries Bryce.

No. I've had enough.

I rush outside and yearn for the peace of the outdoors. It's a little cold, but warm enough. Anyway, Alondra grabbed my red jacket by the door. I look up at the stars. Astraea. It's such a beautiful night.

"Baby, come back," says my dad. He sounds so concerned. I love him so much that that's nearly enough for me to go back.

Alondra, you're inside of me now? Good. But you're not controlling me. Your presence is comforting, teacher. It doesn't feel bad. It's not evil. It feels good. I love you. I miss you so much.

I miss you too, Liam.

I think I'm going to go take a walk. Maybe I'll wander a bit around Maddie's neighborhood. Or walk home. Drive me back home, huh, Bryce? Right now I feel as if I have enough power to fly home on a broomstick.

3

———

THE PENDULUM

WHITE WISPS OF CLOUDS RACE THROUGH BRANCHES OF A TREE canopy as if there's a storm above, but it's a clear, starry night. Occasionally drops of water drip down my face. The wind blows hard, quickly sweeping the water drops from my skin and throwing my long hair to one side, forcing me to brush my bangs back from my eyes. An artificial machine-like buzzing is growing. Then it fades and all becomes still. I feel dark and cold. A bright white light flickers through some leaves. I squint as the whole forest flashes into a single bright white light. Then, as soon as I cover my eyes, the sky blackens again and darkness falls.

Like a pendulum. Back and forth. Back and forth. Sun and moon. Light and dark. Daughter. Mother. *Solus sabbath. Revelare. Crepusculum in perpetuum.*

I'm climbing through thick brush along a hillside now. There's no trail. I don't care. I don't care much about anything at the moment, to be honest.

I make my way down a muddy ditch where a doe is curled up beside its fawns. I pet their soft hides, carefully, so as not to awaken them. Their fur is soft. The fawn's back rises ever so slightly, undulating up and down, with a steady breath. I kneel before the deer, holding my palm softly over her chest. In the moonlight, my breasts and legs are bare, and I'm as naked as the deer.

I leave the deer and follow a path beside a stream, walking away from the flowing water.

Silva. Silva. Umbra. Umbra.

I laugh. I don't know why. I just feel joy tonight. My laughter causes black birds to scatter in the branches above me under a bright half moon. Then I pass an open field and enter another dense forest canopy.

It gets dark. I pull my Book of Shadows, *Broomstick,* out from under my arm and use it as a flashlight, to illuminate the muddy trail. The book holds enough power to light the woods.

As I turn around a very large tree trunk, I notice a violet light emanating under brush. Purple firelight is stewing under the leaves, flickering under my bare feet.

I make my way down the main hallway of my house. The lights are off, but it's bright enough that I can close my book and carry it under my arm. Plastic cups, paper plates with left-over pizza, a few cardboard pizza boxes, crumpled beer cans, chip bags, pieces of a smashed pumpkin, someone's lipstick, and a few bags litter the hallway carpet. Dark, heavy music is blaring from my living room, and I see flickering multicolored lights down the hall. I'm expecting to see a thousand people dancing, but the house is empty.

I pass my dining room. This room is dimly lit by flickering violet candlelight along our dining room table. Two people sit close to each other at the head of the table, quietly eating dinner, not saying a word. They're so quiet, they remind me of ghosts. One's dressed in a black cloak, the other, a guy with thin reddish-brown hair, in a preppy button-down. When the witch lifts her hood, I recognize her face: Alondra. She's wearing black goth makeup with a black star on her forehead. I'm so happy to see her. She looks so much younger than I've seen before.

"*Yatu*, Cadence."

The lovely outdoor forest is vivid through the floor-to-ceiling dining room window. This is the best view of the surrounding woods from our house. On the other side of the table, I see a small violet bonfire blazing. That's weird. We never light fires on our carpet. Well, everything is a bit weird at the moment, to tell you the truth.

I shiver. I'm still naked standing in my dining room. Wasn't I roaming in the woods?

"You asked why we wear gothic makeup and cloaks, and I told you," Alondra says.

"You lied," I object quietly, still staring at the violet bonfire. "You're not real. You all hide behind your makeup."

"I won't ever hide from you. I shall unveil everything to you, Windstorm. One day, all darkness will fade, and your light shall shine forth in Hawthorne. So says prophecy. But be warned: gnosis follows pangs. *Lux alba* for those with feeling, lux *tenebris* for those numb."

There's a flash of light, and Alondra and the visitor are gone. My husband, Bryce, has replaced her, sitting under that same purple candlelight, slaving away at his computer and sifting through papers, like he's been doing into the late hours for the past few months. He uses the dining room as a study so he doesn't disturb my sleep. It's all Kenosha's doing.

"Bryce, what's happening? Am I in a witch wandering?"

I must be. But he doesn't answer. It's like he can't hear me. Or maybe the heavy music, getting louder, is becoming too loud? The machine sound I was hearing has been replaced by heavy rock music shaking the walls of the room.

"Am I in a wandering, Bryce?"

There's laughter coming down our main hallway.

I return to the hallway and follow the laughter. Strangely, I feel unsteady as I walk, dizzy, as if the walls of our hallway are moving. It's as if I'm drunk. I didn't drink that much wine at Maddie's house, did I? Wait… wasn't I at Maddie's house yelling at her mom?

A few candles along the floor flicker purple light over our beige carpet amid more trash. I remember all this trash during my Halloween party a few months ago, but I don't recall the odd violet light. Am I at our Halloween party again? Everything, napkins and plastic bags of trash, is shrouded in this strange color, the same violet as the candles in the dining room and the firelight in the forest.

My living room looks different. All my comfy "normal" brown chairs and white couch have been replaced by vibrant modern fuchsia and mauve. This isn't my taste, it's Alondra's modern eclectic taste. She was always more hip than me. This must be her past. There's a huge mess of paper and spilled cups here too. There's even a red wine bottle on its side, staining our carpet near my bare foot. It's the remnants of a party, but a party is still happening outside. And, boy, I thought my Halloween party was busy. This is nuts. To the beat of heavy rock music, I see complete chaos outside our patio. Hundreds of kids are jumping up and down in my backyard. I've never seen so many bodies out there.

I walk to the sliding glass door for a better look. There's a wood stage where we usually have our central bonfire, and on the stage is this guy shouting into a microphone. Before the stage hundreds of students are slamming into each other in some sort of mosh pit.

Then I turn at the sound of giggling. I'm not alone in the living room. Alondra and that boy I saw in the dining room are leaning close beside each other in a tight embrace beside the sliding glass door. It's a young Alondra again, about my age, kissing that red-haired guy and holding him tight. She's running her hand through his short auburn hair. It reminds me of Bryce's feathery hair—it's so cute.

The sliding glass door is thrown open, and a kid in a gorilla suit falls inside with blood dripping from his nose. Two girls in pirate suits and a woman in a red tank top, baggy camouflage pants, and a long blond wig follow him inside from the patio. I know the girl. She's got bright green eyes and pale skin. It's Alondra. But...isn't she making out with that boy?

I turn to the wall again. Alondra is still there making out with the boy. He has his hand inside her black cloak. I see the curves of Alondra's chest under her cloak as he fondles her breasts.

I turn but the boy with the bloody nose is gone.

No, everyone's gone. Even though the heavy music still blares in my ears, my backyard and patio are empty too.

Except a large violet bonfire.

"It's gonna take us all night to clean this shit, Lee," Alondra says between kisses.

"No doubt," Liam says.

"Hey," Alondra says, backing up and slapping his chest. "You guessed my costume?"

"Yeah, Gwen."

"Did you like my Gwen Stefani outfit?"

"Loved it."

"I knew you would. But you weren't wearing a costume."

"What do you mean? I was wearing your witch cloak."

"That's not a costume, lover."

She unbuttons his shirt. Then he's shirtless, and his chest and stomach are ripped like Bryce's. Between that feathery hair and built abs and pecs, he's hot like Bryce. And his naked chest rubbing against her is arousing me. He lifts Alondra's black cloak, revealing her naked pale body. He caresses her tits again as they kiss, running his fingers along her curves and down over her ass.

I'm blushing. This is wrong. I'm standing in our living room in the past, watching my former teacher, in the nude, making out with a man. It's a different, younger Alondra than I ever knew, but it's still weird. I mean, my teacher was never a prude, she even ran ceremonies in the nude, but, though she was pretty, I never thought of her in any romantic way. I mean, she hated her second husband, Bill Reardon. But it feels really wrong to be watching her being intimate. And yet, I can't keep my eyes off them.

He touches her between her legs, and somehow I feel his touch.

What? How?

I lurch back in shock as he fingers her. He's pressing inside her pussy. No...*I feel* his fingers pressing inside *my* pussy. My heart races, not only in sexual excitement, but also out of fear. He's touching Alondra, but it feels like he's touching me.

Wait...wasn't I walking alone in the forest near Maddie's house?

Umbra. Umbru. Dum vita est, obitus est.

I'm slowly walking, naked, in a forest glade under a bright half-moon. The grass is wet and my bare feet slosh in mud. Above me are lovely bright stars in a clear sky. I shiver, wrap my arms around myself. Something croaks under me. I reach down in the grass and run my fingers along the wet, bumpy skin, of a huge purple frog. Mira once said you can give people warts with frog skin. Maybe I should do that to Kenosha? It croaks. I'm angry at Kenosha, aren't I? Right? Why? Or...wasn't I mad at Maddie's mom, Aunt Jane?

What a strange frog. As I lift it up, it's so huge and heavy, like the size of my chest. Under the white moonlight, it's as purple as a plum. I brush its moist, slimy, bumpy skin along my breasts and nipples. And then I kiss its ass.

~

"Dad's gonna be really pissed," Alondra says with a chuckle between kisses. "The party was more fun, but tomorrow we'll have to clean up."

"Me and our sisters will help you."

They stop yapping. Because they get too heavy with the smooching again. And then...the music stops. It becomes quiet. That's more arousing, because I hear their hands running along soft skin. I hear that wetness—not just their skin, the wetness below. They're naked and preparing for sex. The sounds make me *sooo* aroused. My heart thumps as I listen to the licking of tongues. The lack of music seems to be making these sounds even louder.

"I just loved how you wore our cloak earlier, *High Wizard*."

"A costume, Allie," Liam says between kisses. "I tell you, it was just a costume."

"No, I think it's the real you."

And with that, Allie undoes his belt and zipper. Then she yanks down his pants. She reaches into his underwear, and I see his erect penis.

I feel his cock in my palm. I run my fingers along it and slowly jerk it. He moans. Then he cups my breasts and glides his fingers along my breasts and nipples again. I feel his fingers caressing my soft skin. Then I feel his tongue and soft lips over mine. I run my hands along his hard back and the crack of his ass. His butt flexes as he kisses me harder. Then he runs his fingers down my back. He's exploring *my* soft skin, not Alondra's; *my* breasts, as he runs his fingers over my hard nipples, down my curves, and along the crack of my ass, pressing me closer. Then he kisses me on the lips hard, squeezing me so close, so tenderly.

I stroke his cock again. He moans as I feel his tongue enter my mouth again.

"*Prohibe*," I say weakly, breathless, feeling his tongue in my mouth. "*Prohibe*. Leave this vision." But I kiss his soft lips again. I want to kiss him again. And again. "Leave...Allie in privacy. *Prohibe*." Between kisses, I catch a glimpse of Alondra slowly backing away from Liam and shaking her head.

There's a burst of white light. It's so bright. I'm not holding a frog. I'm holding my book, *Broomstick*, clutching it tightly against my bare breasts. It's my charm, my refuge. Let it cast a shield over whatever's happening.

I turn to my right and see another purple bonfire blazing beside a stream. Trees surround me, their branches and leaves occluding the sky. Did I start these purple flames? Is this my magic or someone else's? And how was I inside my house? Have I wandered that far from Maddie's? Aren't I alone in the forest? Or am I at Maddie's? Or am I back at my Halloween party? Is this Samhain?

The sound of rustling leaves makes me turn. An animal is approaching. No, it's not an animal; it's a person crawling slowly, through the leafy sludge, toward me. There's a rattle and slithering sound, as if there's a snake. When it gets closer, I see a woman's face caked in dark mud, the mud whitening her eyes over gray lips. Aside from shredded clothes hanging from her waist, she's nude, but I can barely make out her breasts under all the filth and grime.

Her white eyes stare at me.

Samhain. Samhain. Samhain!

~

Liam hoists me up in his strong arms. I'm touching my lips to his, as we're French kissing passionately. I want him to hold me like this, to carry me. He's squeezing my ass as he heaves me up. I so desire this. I so want him to make love to me.

Then I feel the pleasure I've been desiring all along. I feel his cock enter me. He lifts me up and down with his cock inside, while squeezing my ass so tight. He's moaning and I'm breathing heavily.

"Fuck me, Lee. Yes, fuck me."

I open my eyes and turn toward the sliding glass door. There's a reflection of a couple making love. But it's not me. It's Allie and Liam.

So why do I feel him? I want him. I desire him so badly.

I close my eyes tight with this desire, using all my magical intent and power to continue to make this happen. I want it to happen. And as I hear the lovemaking, I feel that sensation between my legs. It feels so good. But this is wrong... I close my eyes but still hear our bodies smacking together. Liam's moaning only drives me more. But what about Bryce? Bryce is studying in the dining room. Wasn't he right down the hall?

I crack open an eye. I see a reflection in the glass. Then I shudder. Someone is standing by the entrance to the living room watching us fuck. It's a little girl with pigtails and a short white dress. She has her hand on her mouth, holding back laughter.

I turn away.

My eyes catch another reflection in the sliding glass window. Liam is holding a tan-skinned woman's naked ass, squeezing it tight, with his strong hands pressing into my soft skin. The woman has long dark hair and brown eyes. She's not Alondra, her profile is mine. It's my face lost in total ecstasy. Liam is not fucking Allie now, he's fucking me. And I want him to never stop.

He turns me and throws me hard against the wall. I laugh. He thrusts his cock deep inside me again and again, harder and harder, throwing my whole body again and again against the wall. But...what about next door? What about Bryce?

"Oh, Cadence."

I squint an eye as I feel him sucking my lip. I catch a glimpse of his auburn hair and pale face. Liam's eyes are closed in pleasure too. Then he pulls at my nipple with his teeth, biting me, and runs his tongue along my breast. And he's moaning too, still moving me up and down, fucking me against the wall in my living room.

"Fuck me, Lee. Yes do it. Take me. Fuck me now."

"Oh, Cadence."

Every thrust is pleasure. Every bang against the wall is ecstasy.

"Samhain Witch. Revelare. Revelare!"

I hear this incantation uttered by Alondra's voice. I look back. The girl who was watching us is no longer a girl. Taking her place is a muddy figure hunched over, covered with grime and leaves, with just a few strings of hair. The beast's gray lips are curled in a large grin, and her pearly white eyes are staring at us. She's staring and grinning as Liam and I are fucking. Why are we fucking? I don't care. As terrifying as this beast is, being in this man's arms is so thrilling, so dangerous and exciting, precisely because it's wrong. Precisely because we're being watched...precisely because of...Bryce? Isn't Bryce sitting in—.

Liam sucks and pulls at my lips. He's gentle up there, but not below. I run my hand through his feathery hair and caress his head, which is leaning against my shoulder. With my other hand, my fingers run along his muscular back and over the ripples of his abs. I feel the crack of his ass again, squeezing tightly as he thrusts again and again, pounding me against the wall.

"Oh, Cadence, but maybe—"

"Do it, Lee," I say. "Fuck me, Lee. Don't stop now. Make me cum. Fuck me harder!"

"Oh, Cadence. But we shouldn't."

"No! Fuck me. I'm almost cumming. Fuck me! Fuck me, Lee! Fuck me. Fuck me hard. Do it, Liam! Make me cum."

"Oh, Cadence. Yes. Cadence." But he shakes his head. I almost feel like he's going to let me go.

"*Fuck her now!*" croaks the monster.

Is that the Samhain Witch?

The pleasure is hitting me like a gale. That evil witch's voice echoes around me like a thousand voices as my desire climbs to a crescendo, only building the pleasure even more.

"Yes, do it!" I demand, opening my eyes wide. "Do it! Don't stop, Lee. I'm cumming." He's looking down. I look at the mirror and see my profile being pressed against the wall in the reflection of the window. "Make love to me, Liam. Do it to me now. Fuck me! Fuck me now!"

"Yes, Cadence."

"Oh, yes, Lee. Yes!"

I pull him as close as I can. Then I bounce up and down over him harder than ever.

"Yes, Cadence."

I feel his tongue in my mouth as I cum in his strong embrace.

～

I'm falling. I'm sinking as if I've been dunked in a pool. The half moon sheds just enough light to allow me to see the surface of the water above me. The water is filthy. I move my arms and legs, struggling to swim, but I feel so weak. It's hard to stay afloat. I'm sinking as if I'm in a sink hole, struggling to breathe, over and over, drowning, until finally I feel small pebbles, sticks, and mud between my fingers. I pull myself along the sludge over the edge of the water, fighting to rise, and finally climb over the mud.

~

I'm on my back, in muddy leaves and filth, in that open field in the woods again. The half moon seems as bright as the sun. I feel sick, like I'm going to throw up. Then I'm even sicker when I find my filthy hands between my legs. Was I touching myself? In all this slime and mud! It's then I notice something very heavy and slimy lying on top of my breasts. It's the frog.

Ew, gross! With both hands, I hurl the large animal off me in disgust. It quickly hops off and disappears into the forest.

"Something the matter?" croaks a woman. Those white eyes are staring down at me. The monster-witch is kneeling over me. "What have you done? Did you do something *evil*?"

I close my eyes and turn from her in revulsion. I feel long, sharp fingernails grab my head and throw it back to look upon her muddy face. Her pearly white eyes are unsteady, but they seem to be examining me as if I'm some specimen. Her lips are twitchy. Is she insane? Drugged? I don't know. But I know who she is. The Samhain Witch. The witch who nearly killed me and my friends four months ago after Halloween. How is she here in my woods in Georgia? Near my hallowed grounds? Was my wandering due to her conjuring? Was that sex vision from *her* magic?

"Melanie?" I ask. "Melanie, is that you?"

"Where are your clothes, Cadence Hass-horn?" she asks with a grin. Her curled gray lips look horrifying. "How about your grimoire?"

I look down again. My chest and legs are as filthy as hers. It's like I rolled in the mud. Far worse, I'm holding nothing. It was my book that helped me escape this witch last time.

I quickly turn from her again in revulsion.

"Turn back, damned soul," Melanie says quietly, running those long, sharp nails along my muddy head. "Come now." She pets my cheeks and forehead. "Turn back. Turn back. See what you really are, evil witch. Satan takes you down to Sheol, where you and your coven belong."

I feel so afraid. Defeated. I'm so weak. It's like she's chaining me to the ground.

Then there's a flash of heat and light. The entire field surrounding me ignites into a conflagration of bright purple flames. I smell charring. Is that my body! Oh, my god! My skin! I'm burning! And all the while, that monster is cackling. But she's disappeared. I'm alone in a burning field.

Ardeo! Ardeo! Ardeo!

I don't know what that means, I never know what any of my spells mean, but I shout out those words.

"Yes, speak your Latin charms," the witch says in a whisper. Her voice seems to be everywhere, emanating from the trees. "Enchant me. How 'bout this one, Cadence Hass-horn: *Perdere vita en Inferno.* Speak it. Say it. Repeat it over and over until you can't breathe another word. Fuck it. Just like you just fucked your husband!"

Perdere vita en Inferno. Perdere vita en Inferno. Perdere vita en Inferno. Condemnabetur. Condemnabetur.

4

MORTIFIED, AGAIN

ARTIFICIAL YELLOW LIGHT APPEARS THROUGH LEAVES AND branches. The moon is occluded by clouds now, and it's dark outside. I'm so cold, crouching over, clutching myself tightly, shivering like crazy as a breeze touches my naked skin. Not only am I naked, my skin is wet. I rush barefoot over twigs and mud toward the light, thinking it could be a house. I carefully step over a few branches and leaves and then find a dirt trail. When I recognize a familiar yard full of wild grass with a pile of woods in the center—my yard!—I speed faster. I realize the artificial yellow light is emanating from the living room. My house. When close enough to see through the sliding glass door, I'm surprised to see that my living room is packed with people. Maddie and Bryce are sitting together on the sofa. Damien is leaning against the wall with his hands in his pockets. And sitting across from them are Jane and, worst of all, Dad. Why is Dad here? Wait, he was at Maddie's when I freaked out. Obviously, he must have been too worried to go home to Atlanta.

Maddie spots me first through the glass sliding door. Then she goes nuts screaming. She rushes to the door, but the stupid door's jammed. (It's always jammed.) When she finally pries it open, I jump into her arms.

She throws me off.

"You're so cold, Katie!" She whirls around. "Damie, quick, get me that blanket from the couch. Oh my god, Katie! What's happened?"

My brother rushes over and forces the door wider open. They drape a blanket over me. I'm still shivering like crazy.

I'm grabbed by someone else from behind.

"Cadence!" says Bryce. "Oh Cadence, thank god, Cadence. Thank god you're okay. We were so worried." I grab for him, wanting to hold him tightly in my arms, but he backs away from my icy body too. "What's happened, baby? What happened…"

Then comes Dad. Jane, standing by a lounge chair, doesn't move. I remember our fight.

"Help me upstairs," I say quietly to Bryce. My teeth are chattering and my whole body's shaking.

"We need to talk, Windstorm." Kenosha is standing by the hallway. I didn't even notice she was here. She's wigless, bald, in her forest green cloak, looking like a total witch. I glance at Dad. Weirder, Kenosha is not alone. Sitting in one of our wooden dining room chairs is a frail white-haired woman in a shiny indigo cloak.

"Not now," Bryce snaps, shaking his head. He wraps an arm around me again. "Come upstairs, Cadence."

"She's in no condition to talk to you now, Kenosha," Aunt Jane echoes.

Bryce takes me in his arms and leads me down our main hallway. My friends and family are murmuring like crazy behind me as we climb the stairs.

"I need to shower," I say to Bryce, teeth still vibrating, as we enter our bedroom.

"Oh, Cadence, I've been so worried about you. We kept

thinking of ways to find you. Kenosha even suggested casting a spell."

"Why is Dad here?"

"He knows. He knows everything after dinner at Maddie's. He knows about our magic now. He saw your eyes turn green, Cadence. Remember? Or were you even aware Alondra was inside you?"

I remember.

But I don't say anything. I'm too busy shivering.

"Dad doesn't care," Bryce continues, "as long as you're all right. He was just so worried. We were all worried something horrible happened to you in the forest. We even called the police to search for you. You walked all the way back from Maddie's house? What sort of wandering is this, babe? That's miles away. And what was happening at Maddie's house, anyway? I've never seen you say a single bad thing to Aunt Jane." When I'm still silent, he quickly adds, "Forget it. Just forget about anything. I'm so glad you're safe now."

"I'm scared, Bryce. I don't feel like I have control. I don't know if Alondra is still inside me or not. And the Samhain Witch is attacking us again."

"The Samhain Witch? How? It's not even Halloween."

"I don't know. But I saw her. But... I'm okay, Bryce."

I'm really not okay, to tell you the truth, but I don't want to worry him more.

"How did she attack you?"

I don't answer. And he doesn't pry. Instead he leads me to the bathroom and turns on a light. I see the familiar elegant brass swan-neck faucets and marble shower in our lovely tile bathroom. You must admit, Alondra had style.

But then I catch a glimpse of my face in the mirror. What the hell? My cheeks and forehead are coated in mud and leaves. I don't even recognize myself. I look hideous...like a monster. Like...the Samhain Witch.

When I turn back toward our bedroom, I catch Bryce's expression. He's got bags under his red eyes. He hasn't been sleeping. Or has he been crying?

"I didn't mean to say all those horrible things to Aunt Jane."

"She knows it wasn't you, but that worried us even more. You've been missing for three days, Cadence."

Three days!

I drop the blanket on the tile floor. I'm too filthy to be wearing anything, and it's warmer in our bedroom. Then I walk over to our floor-to-ceiling bedroom window. I still hear our guests downstairs talking like crazy. And I'm still shivering a little, but I'm warming up.

Actually, I feel different from when I was outside. Not only am I warmer, I feel stronger. In our backyard, for the first time ever, I felt scared. No, worse. I felt ashamed. Humiliated, just like my first lecture, but far worse. Last year, I was afraid of that evil witch Enora and her power, worried she would kill me or my friends. The Samhain Witch is different. She didn't make me scared, she made me feel humiliated. Why?

Was it even Melanie? Bryce is right. I thought she was called the Samhain Witch because she only appears on Halloween. Maybe some other witch, like Enora, was conjuring an image of her?

Not only that, whoever she was, she attacked me on my hallowed ground. All the woods in these parts of Hawthorne are my hallowed grounds. My home. I'm supposed to feel great power on my own land.

I look back and Bryce is smiling sweetly. His smile almost appears sultry. Is it my naked body? Am I turning him on? It doesn't excite me. It only reminds me of my vision of cheating on him. I quickly turn back to the window.

There's a large violet bonfire lit in the middle of our yard. That's strange.

"Are you...Cadence *now*?"

"Yes, Bryce," I say with a nod, still staring down at our yard.

He touches my shoulder but then quickly jerks his fingers back. "Your skin is still icy cold."

"It's better that you don't touch me. I feel dirty."

"You want to shower?" he asks.

I nod.

But not yet. I just want to stand here overlooking our backyard. He stands beside me, and we both sort of stare out at our forest through our large bedroom window. It's pretty, but I don't care for the violet bonfire.

I hear louder yapping downstairs. All my friends are still worried to death over me.

"I'm just happy you're safe," Bryce says.

And sweet Bryce kisses my cheek. Then he kisses the back of my neck. Is my magic arousing him? Probably. I just had a wandering. Witch wanderings always fill me with sexual energy. Usually a wandering attracts men, and I love attacking my husband ravenously and making love to him during one. But...not now.

Why not now? I don't want him to touch me. I want him to leave me alone. I just want to wash off all this filth. I feel so dirty. Why?

Maybe it's because you had sex with someone else?

5

CONFESSION TIME

It's snowing. The last snow of the season, I suppose. It's almost April, you know. But the funny thing is, as I sit by the window of the university coffee shop, enjoying the view of all that fluffy ice outside, I feel happy. Normally, I don't like snow, but this Saturday my bestie's meeting with me. And boy, do I need a latte with Maddie right now.

It's been a week since my meltdown at her house. I still haven't apologized to her mom. Nor have I had that "talk" with Kenosha. But Kenosha's already sticking her nose into our business, telling Bryce not to do anything related to witchcraft on behalf of my condition. She's worried I'll have another wandering. And Bryce—though I love him to death—is acting so strange, as if I'm pregnant or something. No, I'm not kidding, like everywhere I go he keeps texting and calling me, asking if I'm okay.

Maddie's late, as always. That's okay. I can sip tea and enjoy the view of our campus below.

You know, if there's one thing I can tell you about Hawthorne University, it's that we've got trees. And I don't mean like a group circling a garden, or one or two beautifying the curtilage in your front yard, I'm talking about full-on lush canopies shadowing *everything*, wherever you walk in town, so thick as to occlude the clouds or rays of sunlight. It's as if you're in a constant embrace with nature. And I love that. But I also hate it. Because all those canopies of trees can feel restricting. Dark. Like an all-encompassing mother. Like... Alondra.

I take another sip of my green tea latte over that.

Anyway, the view is absolutely to die for. Even though it's chilly, the sky is clear, and I can still enjoy the view from behind the glass.

I take another sip.

Beyond the field is our main campus walkway with brick buildings on both sides, and right now I see a few students braving the weather, carrying books under their arms, with backpacks slung over their shoulders. I have to squint. (I've been doing that a lot lately. Yep, after too much reading, Teaching Assistant Cadence Wallace needs to wear glasses.)

"Hey Ms. Wallace," hollers a blond kid after entering the café.

I turn and wave.

Then I just stare at the small white porcelain cup on the table. It was steamy when I bought it. Why was I stupid enough to buy Maddie a drink? Since when has Madison Taylor ever been on time?

"Hey Katesy!"

I jump from my chair and, before you know it, she's in my arms. Unlike my professor look this morning, she's got on goth lipstick and eyeshadow. The only really witchy thing is my long black fingernails.

We sit back down, and I gesture to her cup on the table.

"What'd'ya get me?"

"Something to keep you from stealing."

"Oh, I gave that up long ago, babe," she says, shooing me with a hand. She takes a sip. "Hmm...it's cinnamonny but...cold.

Real cold. Shit, I'm so sorry I'm late, Cadence. Must have been hard for you. I know you like to get up at, like, eleven."

"Hi, Ms. Wallace," hollers a girl with long blond hair holding two books. She's got on a red skirt and a sweater with golden letters.

"Ms. Wallace, huh," Maddie says. "And a sorority snoot, no less. I love it when they call you that."

I shrug.

"So, how're you doing?" Maddie asks, suddenly turning grave. "Damie and I are so worried about you. I told him we should have stayed over at your house or something."

"I'm fine."

She studies my eyes. Then she shakes her head slowly. She sips more of her drink, but almost spits it out.

"Damn, Katie, I can't, I just can't do this. I just can't. Are you trying to bring back old habits? It's cold, like outside. I'm about ready to do some good ole stealing."

"You were late. And you better not."

"Right." Maddie scoots her cup away from her. "So? Have you seen the Samhain Witch again?"

I shake my head.

"Thank god. What about Alondra?"

It's funny, because she asks as if she doesn't really want to know.

"Everything's back to normal."

"Sure." She slowly nods, seeming to not believe me.

"I'm fine, Maddie."

"Kates, when I flipped last year, I needed help. I'd never have asked anyone for it. It's obvious Melanie is casting a spell on you, just like Enora did to me last year. I learned you can't shut down about this stuff. You have to bring everything out into the open."

I just shake my head.

"Well, I hope you're not really going through with a lecture tomorrow, *Mrs. Wallace.*"

"I am. It's my job and it's my make-up lecture."

"Your job is to be a graduate student and assistant to your metaphysical history professor, not to run lectures. I don't think you should do it, and neither does Bryce. What happens if you suddenly become Alondra onstage?"

I laugh because that sounds so stupid.

"Could happen. I also don't think the coven should meet on Friday. Your brother and I are seriously freaked out after we heard you saw the Samhain Witch again. Honestly, Katie, Damien and I couldn't sleep for days after going to that house last Halloween. I don't want anything to do with Samhain. Shit, I even hate that name. I mean, let's just call it Halloween, 'kay? Maybe call her the Halloween Witch?"

"I know, Maddie. I know."

"I don't think you do, *Alondra*. No lectures and no sabbath. Okay?"

"No." I shake my head. Then I drink more tea. "No, Maddie. I'm doing the lecture. I really want to do it."

"Cadence, even Mom thinks you shouldn't lecture."

"Maddie," I snap, "why should I care what your mom thinks?" Out of habit, I throw my head back to push back my long hair, but then I realize I'm being stupid, with my hair in a professor bun. "I've been thinking... shouting at your mom wasn't totally wrong. I mean, I love her and all, but... I mean, she should have told us about what was going on during our sophomore year. We could have avoided so many problems with you, Bryce, even—"

"Don't you think she knows that?" Then she leans forward and searches my eyes. "Is this Alondra talking now?"

"Cut it out! No. Maddie, I love your mom, but I think she deserved to be yelled at. That's all I'm saying."

"She'd be the first to admit to it. She's not happy about what happened, but talking about it only makes her more depressed. I really don't want you mentioning it to her again."

"Your mom, depressed? I don't believe that. That's like you being depressed. You two can never be sad."

She grimaces and raises her cup in a toast. But then she almost spits her drink out again.

"Fuck. Fuck, no, babe! No. This is *sooo* gross. Sorry. No, no. I can't do this. I'm gonna go get a mystery drink for old time's sake. It'll be fun. You can only blame yourself."

"You better not."

"You know better, Cadence," she says with a laugh, raising a finger. "Since when am I ever on time? It's like expecting you to get up early in the morning."

She walks over to the counter. And then...she's doing it. She goes right up to the counter and swipes someone's to-go cup without checking the label. Then she sips it, gloating at me over her kleptomania.

"I don't think that's yours, miss," I loudly blurt.

Maddie's eyes grow huge.

"It's okay, Ms. Wallace," says a nerdy boy with glasses and a red backpack standing next to Maddie. "I think that was mine. I'll just order it again."

I grunt, jump up, and say to the kid, "what'dya order?"

"Just a small cup of Kona coffee." Serves Maddie right. Maddie hates regular coffee.

I get up and holler to a gray-haired woman in a red and gold apron behind the counter, "Miss, can you grab me another Kona, please? I accidentally took this student's drink. You can charge me."

The nice lady nods.

I tell you, this woman is like a fixture at our coffee house. I've seen her here ever since I first arrived at Hawthorne University.

I wait with the kid behind me. I shouldn't have to wait long because she just needs to pour brewed coffee. Looking back at our table, I see Maddie brooding, looking like she's ready to storm out. I suppose I trapped her. She can't very well hand the kid back his coffee. When she meets my gaze, she slowly mouths the word "*bitch*" and then she sticks up her middle finger.

The lady behind the counter hands me the cup of Kona with a smile.

Then I hear that nerdy kid behind me say, "So kind, Cadence. Such a white light shines over you, dearest daughter. But I thirst, Windstorm. I thirst. When are you going to bring my husband back to Hawthorne?"

I whirl around. Right before me is not that nerdy boy with a red backpack, but a witch in a black cloak. Alondra. Here and now, like, Alondra is *really* here. I tell you Alondra, my beloved teacher who died two years ago, is standing right before me taking the place of that young boy. She's not a young Allie, this is the Alondra I remember as my teacher. Her emerald eyes, under the bright lights, gaze deeply into mine.

"Where's Liam, Cadence? Why won't you find him and bring him back to me? Hawthorne is in danger, and you're running out of time."

Then she disappears.

Replacing her form is the kid. He's rushing out of the coffee house. I look down. My slacks are wet. The cup of coffee fell from my hand and burst open over my white tennis shoes. I think it fell on that poor kid. I snatch some napkins and hopelessly wipe my stained white tennis shoes.

Then I gaze back at our table. Madison is still sulking, totally oblivious to everything that happened. She's just staring out the window at our campus, below the hill, stewing as snowflakes lightly hit the glass.

"You never apologized to Mom," Maddie says, still staring outside, as I take a seat. "I suppose she hates you no more than she hates me right now." She folds her arms. "You fucked the whole thing up, Cadence. How can you rat on your bestie like that? This isn't even worth drinking now. I hate plain coffee, you know."

She turns from the window with a big grin. She's not really mad, she's playing. But when she finally looks over, her eyes bulge.

"What's the matter?" she asks quietly.

I shake—not my head, my whole body.

"God, what is it, babe?" Maddie grabs my arm. "What the hell is the matter?"

I put my head in my hands.

"Cadence, tell me."

I shake my head.

"Cadence, you have to tell me."

"Alondra. I just saw her. It was just Alondra."

"*Just Alondra?* What the hell do you mean, *just Alondra.* Alondra died, Cadence. Like, you saw her *here*?"

"Yeah," I say looking up. "Just now, Alondra was standing right in front of me. It made me spill a cup of coffee on that poor student. But she wasn't transparent like a ghost, Maddie. She literally was standing in front of me."

"I thought she was inside you?"

"*She's everywhere, Maddie!*" I cry, dropping my head in my hands. "Shit! She keeps telling me over and over to bring Liam back to Hawthorne. I don't get why. You remember how everything that happens to us somehow appears magically cataloged in my Book of Shadows, *Broomstick*?"

"Yes, but I'd rather you not talk about that."

"Well, lately, I don't see anything chronicled in my diary. I see Liam's name written over and over and over again. Either it's Alondra telling me how much she loves him, or it's just his name stuck in my head. I see his name written over and over and over and over again on every page in Alondra's handwriting."

~

Liam. Liam.

~

"Who's Liam?"

"I told you at your house. Liam Johansen. Remember I asked your mom during dinner? Alondra's first husband. Remember, that's what I raged about?"

"Oh, yeah," she says, rolling her eyes. "It's so weird that Alondra never spoke about him."

"But we met him. Remember? At Beltane."

"Why yes, Cadence, I sure do remember Beltane. You told Mom what you swore you would never tell her. I sure do remember. *Do you remember me telling you to never tell Aunt Jane?*"

"Yeah, sorry about that. Well, I'm obsessed with him. Maddie, one night, Bryce saw me writing his name in the book. I don't usually need to write in the book because, you know, the words appear from my head." She squirms again. "Sorry. I know you don't want me to talk about it."

"Yeah, please don't."

"Well, Bryce was gazing over my shoulder in bed one evening and saw me writing Liam's name in my book. I kept scribbling it over and over and over again. It was appearing on the blank pages in Alondra's handwriting."

"I thought you told me there's no more room left in your book."

"It's a fucking magic book, Maddie!"

A couple and a student studying at two nearby tables turn. Maddie smiles and puts her finger to her lips. "Careful, you're teaching assistant *Ms. Wallace*, remember?"

"I must have written fifty pages with just his name," I say, hitting the table. "Liam, Liam, Liam. I'm completely obsessed with Liam. Why? Maddie, it's almost as if I have a crush on him. But I'm married. But it's not even me, it's Alondra. I think. I think it's Alondra. I don't even know. I think she never lost her love for her first husband, you know, and, in some ways, that's even more tragic. But I don't even think that's why Alondra's asking Lee to come here. I really think her spirit is trying to help us. Just like when I attacked your mom, it wasn't only to get all that bitterness off my chest, it was to get your mom to help us. Alondra's spirit is doing everything she can from the spirit world to tell us how to fix Hawthorne. Right now, that means getting Liam to come here. Maybe for his magic? Maybe because of my love for him? I don't know. And her spirit just appeared asking why I haven't brought him yet."

"This is what I'm talking about. You have to share with me. You can't keep all this inside."

"I'm sharing," I say, opening my arms wide. "Okay! I am sharing it all with you right now."

"Okay. Quiet the hell up, Cadence. I got it."

"So? Does it matter? I just poured coffee over some poor kid seeing her. I just wish she'd leave me alone."

I bury my face in my hands again. I hear her scoot her chair close. She rubs my back.

"I'm sharing, Maddie," I say as she keeps rubbing my back. "I'm sharing. Okay? I don't think it's making things any better."

"I know, babe. It's okay."

"I can't sleep," I say, shaking my head. "You said you and Damie haven't been able to sleep for days, I haven't slept in weeks. And all of this is messing up Bryce really bad. Not only is he up nearly all night working, when he finally does come to bed, he can't sleep."

"It's okay."

"No. There's more. This isn't even why I wanted to talk with you this morning."

Then I feel afraid, but it's not over tomorrow's lecture. I've been afraid of this all morning too. I'm scared of confiding in my best friend what I've been wanting to tell her all along.

"When I had my witch wandering, something really strange happened."

"That's why it's called a witch wandering, Cadence," she quips with a laugh. "Aside from you losing your clothes, something weird always happens."

I don't laugh with her. And now I don't really want to tell her.

"Sorry. What happened?" she asks.

"I can't tell Bryce. I don't know who else to tell. It's so horrible. But I want to tell you. Just swear that you won't tell anybody. Okay?"

"What is it, babe? We're besties. You can tell me anything. Even after you ratted me out and forced me to drink cold lattes and plain coffee." Then she jumps up. "Wait a minute. I'm gonna at least get some free sugar with this shit. Just hold on one second with your secret, 'kay?"

I nod.

Then I look down at the field through the window while I wait for my friend. The green lawn is turning white as snowflakes continue to fall. Ice is also covering the main drag of campus. I quickly turn away. I remember having looked down at the main thoroughfare and seen Alondra's ghost a few times. If that were to happen now, I don't know if I could take it.

Maddie sits back down. She opens a small bag of sugar and pours it in her coffee. Then she wrinkles her nose, shrugs, and sips it. "At least it's hot. Okay. Ready. Go. What's up, babe?"

"In my wandering, I saw Liam."

"So?"

"What I'm about to tell you, Maddie, you must never tell anyone."

She just nods. Then she wrinkles her nose again, sipping coffee. "Maybe it needs cream? Never mind. Got it. Go. I won't tell anybody—even though you told my mom about Beltane."

"Maddie!"

"I won't tell, okay? Just go ahead and tell me already."

"Well, during my trance, I saw Liam and Alondra in my living room. This was before I saw Melanie, the Samhain Witch. I think it wasn't just Alondra inside me driving me to see her, I think it was Melanie. The witch was casting a nasty spell on me. Well, Alondra and Liam started getting intimate. You know, like some heavy kissing."

"Ew, gross."

"What do you mean?"

"Kates, Alondra was like our mom."

"Well, she was very young in the vision. Younger than you and I."

"Okay." She gestures for me to carry on. But now I really don't feel like telling her.

"You know how Alondra possesses me, right? Well, Alondra and Liam not only kissed. They had sex."

"So? I mean, gross, but so? So you saw them have sex?"

"No. You don't understand. I had sex."

"Huh?"

"This is...so embarrassing." I put my head in my hands again and take a deep breath. "I had sex with him. I was channeled into Alondra's body in the vision. I ended up having sex with Liam in our living room, in our living room from the past. All the while, Bryce was studying in the dining room right down the hall. I know my vision of Bryce was in present time, but in my trance, I saw him working in one room while I... *had...*

sex... with Liam in the other room. I knew he was just down the hall. And I felt everything. I felt Liam, I tell you, inside of me. Through magic, it was as real as if I really had sex with him. I have never been with another man, you know."

Maddie smiles real wide. I think she's holding back laughter. "You're so freaky, babe. Did I ever tell you that? You always say I'm fun, but you're completely wackoville."

"Maddie, you're not helping."

"Sorry," she says with a chuckle. "So what? It was just a vision. That was obviously Melanie's spell to make you feel horrible."

"I cheated on my husband."

"You saw a vision," Maddie says, shaking her head.

"No, I had sex with him."

"No, you were in a witch wandering. You had a vision. At least...wait, it was a vision, right? It was during the wandering?"

"Yes, it happened in my vision," I say, nodding. "But, no. Do you remember Bryce's first incubus spell? We both felt everything when we had sex even though I was in a bathtub alone at your house. That was a magic vision too. What if Liam felt me from the Samhain Witch's magic spell for real?" I put my head in my hands again as Maddie rubs my back. "Bryce was studying in the dining room next door, Maddie. And the thing is, I knew he was there. I didn't care. In fact, it drew me even more to Liam. Because it was wrong. It wasn't only that Alondra loved him and was attracted to him. *I was attracted to him,* Maddie."

I stop. I almost grab more of my drink, but I decide not to. Something tells me it's not going to taste as good.

"That's what you've been wanting to tell me?" Maddie asks. "I don't get it. That was in your wandering. It was in a trance created by the Samhain Witch. You didn't cheat on Bryce. You barely knew what the hell was going on."

"I knew what was happening, Maddie. I knew exactly what

was going on. It was wrong, I felt everything, and I wanted it all to happen. You have to...you have to swear to never tell Bryce. I really don't want to hurt him."

"That's why you would never do this. If you hadn't been in a trance and this boy was in the living room with you, you would never have done that to Bryce. That witch made you do it so you'd feel horrible. And it's working."

"No, I wanted him, Maddie," I say, shaking my head. "No, I wanted him whether Bryce was there or not. And the thing is, I still want him. I'm not entirely sure if that desire is Alondra's or mine. I think it's mine. I'm so confused. Honestly, don't tell your mom either, but I'm still furious at her too. Alondra should be, not me. I've never been mad at Aunt Jane in my life. But for some reason, I'm mad at her."

"Oh, babe," she says, shaking her head, "don't lecture tomorrow. You sound sick. Did you tell all this to Kenosha?"

"I'm not going to tell her about cheating on Bryce!"

"Cadence," she cries, leaning forward, "stop saying *cheating*, all right? Don't you know that witch wants to hurt us. What better way than to mess with your relationship with your husband. Enora did that to you before, remember? The dean texted Damien to tell you that she wanted to speak with you. Kenosha said she's been texting you all week, but you keep ignoring her texts. You really need Kenosha's help. She can help you."

"I hate her, Maddie. She humiliated me during my first lecture."

"She even supposedly brought some powerful witch from England to help you," Maddie says with a shrug. "Didn't you see her at your house? She's named Agnes. Her witch name is Andromeda. You need to tell this Andromeda about what happened too. They can help you."

"I'm not telling anyone but you about having sex with Liam."

"Why not? Was it a trance or wasn't it? I don't understand, Katie. Was it?"

"It was a trance," I say with a nod. "But I felt and wanted everything. And I don't know if Liam was there for real or not."

"Did you tell Bryce?"

"Are you nuts! I told you, I don't want to hurt him. Only you know."

"If you tell your husband, he'll tell you it was a trance. And he will help you. I keep telling you, because it happened to me. When you're under the influence of a curse you don't want to share, it's part of the dark magic. But you have to break the secrecy and tell people. We all love you. Being open is the only way we can help. Come on, babe. You need Kenosha's help. Kenosha is the only one who can help you, whether you like her or not. You told me that's why Alondra brought her here."

"Only Liam and Alondra can help me," I say, shaking my head. "That's the other thing I wanted to tell you. I think this is the whole reason Alondra is inside me. Allie wants me to bring Lee back here to Hawthorne. Somehow, only he can fix this—not any witch, including Kenosha. So I'm going to go get him."

"So you can have sex with him!" asks Maddie. She looks around. She was a bit too loud this time. Then she says more quietly, "To have sex, Cadence? For real? Come on, babe, you're acting totally out of your mind. Do you know how weird you're sounding? You don't want to tell anybody but me about your sexual encounter, you're not sure if it was real, you're worried over your marriage, but you want to go meet this guy again, this time in person. It sounds like you want him here in Hawthorne for *you*, not Alondra."

Of course I've totally lost my fucking mind, so I'm not sure. You would turn nutso too if all the shit from the past three years happened to you. Too bad you can't talk to me and tell me what I should do.

"How can I help you, babe?" Maddie asks.

"Come with me to Jersey. I can't reach him, so I'm going to show up at his front door. I don't know what else to do. If I don't, I think Alondra's going to enjoy pestering me even more, maybe forever. I was going to invite Bryce, but with Alondra's strange romantic shit…"

"But are you going there to be alone with this other guy or not?"

"No!" I say quickly, shaking my head. "Of course not."

"Maybe Bryce should go with you."

"He can't. Anyway, I've already asked. He's too busy being overworked by the dean. Look, I don't even know Liam. And I would never hurt Bryce. I love Bryce. It's Alondra inside me, I tell you. I mean, her ghost just told me again, a second ago, to get him."

"But, Katie, you keep telling me you're not sure."

"I need to see him to figure out what Alondra wants. I have to do something to end all this. I'm completely obsessed. Kenosha wants me not to teach, but honestly the lecture tomorrow is a nice distraction from thinking about this guy every waking moment."

"It sounds like a crush, babe. Like some weird, wicked love spell from the Samhain Witch. I don't get why you would want to see him when you keep telling me that you don't want to hurt Bryce."

"Crush or not, I think he's the only man who can help Hawthorne."

"Okay, whatever you need, whatever it takes, Cadence, I'm here for you. If you really think seeing Liam will help, I'll go to New Jersey. Sure. You know our whole coven is spooked. Frida and Helen confided in me they're not only worried for you, they're scared for us. I even spoke with Mira. She's thinking of dropping everything and visiting you in Hawthorne. All of us think the Samhain Witch is out to harm us. Mira thinks that with all your suffering, you must be the focal point of Melanie's raging over the town, because you're our leader. Anyway." She gives a big grimace. "I'd love to go. I've never been to New York City."

"New Jersey. We'd be going to Jersey, Maddie, not New York City."

"Well, if I'm going, we can do a quick stop in Manhattan, right? It's right next door, you know."

"Sure, Maddie," I say with a laugh. "Okay."

"Babe, but with everything you've said about Liam, I still don't agree."

"I believe it's the only way to fix what's happening. I haven't spoken to Kenosha because she still thinks I'm possessed. She doesn't even get that Alondra's spirit is trying to help me. Even now, after she freaked me out, I believe Alondra is a positive force, Maddie. She's not our enemy. It's really her soul trying to help us. I think she thinks Liam can help."

"When do you want to go?"

"This week. Can you take two to three days off?"

She nods.

"Thanks, Maddie. I feel like you're the only one I can confide in. I didn't want to hurt Bryce with all this stuff. You better not tell him."

"We're besties," she says with a shrug. "Anyway, we might be sisters-in-law pretty soon." She quickly puts up her palm, probably seeing my expression. I even feel the warmth in my cheeks. "Just calm down, Cadence." And she laughs. "I'm feeling better now, even after you infernally told on me. Except the coffee still sucks. I think I'm gonna go steal another."

"You better not."

6

———

WHAT IS EVIL?

I'M ONSTAGE, SAFELY BEHIND MY WOODEN PODIUM, IN OUR MAIN lecture hall ready to attempt another masterful debacle. I look like a total professor. My hair is tied in a bun again, and I have on a black sports jacket with a white blouse and black pants. And, behold, three hundred kids are staring at me again. So are Bryce and Kenosha, in the front row. Kenosha looks sharp, elegantly dressed with her curly wig. Bryce looks nervous, Kenosha looks angry. Kenosha insisted that Bryce have me rest until the coven could come up with a plan to shield us from the Samhain Witch. I said I'm feeling better. (I'm not feeling better, okay, but don't you be telling anybody.)

I look down at my notes on the podium. There aren't any. I brought my book, *Broomstick,* instead. I hold back laughter. Usually there's writing, but the pages are blank now. At least they don't have you-know-who's name.

I miss you, Lee.

I spoke too soon. The words appear before my eyes, in black ink on a white page, in Alondra's handwriting. I just can't hold back laughter over that. My laugh is heard through all the speakers in the hall.

I open one of Allie's old lecture folders on my laptop screen. I've copied her entire hard drive onto my PC. I flip through all the familiar pictures until I get to a red screen with a black backward pentagram. Then I shine that on the large monitor behind me.

And, lo and behold...it works!

"Can anyone tell me what this symbol means?"

Kenosha jumps from her seat and rushes to the stage. She's furious over something, I don't know what. When she approaches, I quickly walk center stage and gesture with an extended arm at the screen behind me.

"Hmm? Can anyone tell me?"

Kenosha slowly backs down a step.

"A pentagram, Ms. Wallace," a student shouts.

"Right. A pentagram. But this one is upside down, isn't it? A satanic upside down pentagram. An occult five-pointed star that supposedly represents the devil. Let's talk about that. What makes it evil?"

I change the slide to a sketch of an ancient Babylonian priest. Kenosha returns to her seat, but she looks crazy. She keeps whispering something in Bryce's ear. He keeps shushing her.

"The ancient god Marduk was worshipped with the five-pointed star in Sumeria five thousand years ago. Ancient Sumeria is the first known civilization, existing somewhere between four thousand and two thousand BCE, consisting of the southern lands between the Tigris and Euphrates in Mesopotamia." An ancient map pops up on the screen. "Some say Eden from the book of Genesis resided there. To orient you, this is now Southern Iraq. Later, the lands of Sumer would become part of ancient Babylonia.

"Anyway, we've discovered the pentagram on Sumerian pottery. Would Sumerians have cared if the symbol was backward? Maybe while someone was pouring out drinking water?"

A couple students laugh. "No, it wasn't until the occultist Aleister Crowley, in the twentieth century, made it famous by turning the symbol backward for his cult practices in Thelema. It was actually right side up on the sketch by Eliphas Levi of Baphomet in the nineteenth century. Later Anton LaVey used the upside down symbol, in the 1960s, as the Sigil of Baphomet and the symbol for his Church of Satan. In other words, this symbol's familiar darkness and fear was *created* recently, in the twentieth century. It was not even known as a devil symbol before. Speaking of upside down, what of an upside down cross?"

I press the remote button again to change the slide to a simple image of an upside down cross.

"Most of you, without any research, know this symbol represents the devil. But did you know that the upside down cross is worshipped today by some Christians? Some say the Apostle Peter did not want to sully the glory of Jesus, so when he faced death, he humbly asked that he be crucified upside down. Was the Apostle Peter evil? Of course not. It was taken as a great symbol of humility, meaning that humans could never achieve the divine grace of God. How did the symbol become evil? We created this evil association in our minds."

I look down in thought. It's quiet. I've totally got all the kids' attention. Maybe I should just bow and get the hell off the stage before I screw everything up?

"What I was trying to say last time...during my first lecture, which I botched..." More students laugh. "Is that this meta-physical history class is very special for my husband and me. Dr. Johansen was such a powerful mentor at Hawthorne, not only in presentation, or details, but in her depth. She taught me so much. Well, back when I was an undergraduate student like you, she had us write an essay on what makes these symbols evil. But I've been thinking of a different approach. A different question for all of you. Not what makes a *symbol* evil but, more simply, *what is evil?*"

I press the button again. I'm doused in red light from the slide shining behind me. This is Alondra's famous slide of the drawing by Eliphas Levi of Baphomet, a horned hermaphrodite beast with wings, snakes at his crotch, and one hand up and another down. The crimson background creates a menacing effect. Alondra was a queen at showmanship back when she lectured here, you know.

"What is evil? Is this evil? The pentagram on his, or her, forehead is right side up, like I told you. So is this devil *good*?"

Kenosha goes nuts. She jumps up again but, this time, my professor and hubby, Bryce, yanks her elbow down. She starts raging in his ear again. Then she folds her arms and falls back in her chair in a huff, glaring at me.

"What is evil?" I repeat, grinning down at her. "If any one of you can answer that, I believe you will have unlocked one of the greatest mysteries of life. And, perhaps, you can end all our suffering and sin."

How 'bout that, Alondra? You never thought of that one.

"Evil is not just fear," I answer. "Many of you were taught to fear God. God is not evil. Evil is not hidden, for mystery and discovery are wonders of life. Any of you gone on vacation? Did you go to see something *hidden? Occult?* Evil is not pain. If evil were pain, then childbirth would be evil, and babies are one of the most wonderful things on Earth. Yet all of us seem to know what evil is, right?

"Perhaps evil is simply murder? But every country on Earth engages in war. Is murder okay if it's done in an orderly fashion with uniforms? At the greatest extreme, war fights racism, extermination, rape, and torture. If the United States had not fought World War II, perhaps all of us would have been ruled under a swastika in a society exterminating other races. (Ah, the swastika, there's another symbol stolen and transfigured in the twentieth century). So not all war is bad. Or is it? Philosophically, then, when I ask you what evil is, there's not a simple answer. I posit that it's a metaphysical conundrum."

I change the slide to just a dim yellow light and shut my mouth. Then I stand there at center stage and look out at a sea of faces. Honestly, I'm about ready to pat myself on the back. I'm not funny or casual like Alondra. I'm intense. But no one's heading out the back doors.

"So...*what is evil?*"

A few students near the front row raise their hands. I point to one of them.

"The absence of civility, Ms. Wallace," suggests a guy in the front row. "The absence of law. Sin and lack of God is evil."

"The lack of law and order?" I ask with a nod. "That is often what Western religions teach. Law is a foundation in the Torah, Quran, and Christian Bible. But, looking at these Western religions, before their fall from the Garden of Eden, what law did Adam and Eve live by? It seems they lived in eternal blissful ignorance. Thereby, whatever actions taken before their fall were excused of sin. In fact, the only law in the garden was to not eat from the tree of knowledge. So was the realm devoid of law in Eden evil? With such logic, Eden before the fall would be considered evil. Right?" I shake my head. "No."

The next slide is a picture of a snake. I look down at Kenosha. What's her deal? She looks ready to jump up on stage and strike me in the face.

"We all have a sense of what evil is." *Maybe it's the bitch sitting under me?* "A mass murderer. A rapist. A torturer. These are evil people doing evil things. Sure. But a quick, simple answer still eludes me."

"Evil is doing what's wrong, Ms. Wallace," a girl shouts out midway down the auditorium. I recognize Jennifer from my study group. "Secretive—yes. Dark and frightening. That's what evil is."

"I disagree. I think good can be dark and frightening too." I mean, try living with friends that you love in a dark witch cult at Hawthorne University. "But I do believe evil exists. What do you think, Dr. Trent?" But before the bitch can speak, I say, "If Bryce, I mean, Dr. Wallace, will permit me, I think we should all write an essay answering this question. I'm sure Alondra would have wanted that. I'm plainly asking you what evil is. No symbols. Not even history. But you can use history to back up your argument if you want an 'A'". People laugh. "I think it'd be a good exercise, if our professor will permit it?"

Bryce nods with a very big smile. He is in complete contrast to the woman scowling beside him.

Done. There, Kenosha, go top that.

I mosey back to the podium, wrapping my arms around myself. I look down and move my black fingernail over the touch pad again to clear it for Bryce. Carrying my Book of Shadows under my arm, I hand the microphone on my collar back to Bryce. Then I nod to the audience before I walk down the steps.

The lecture hall goes crazy, erupting in applause.

7

———

THE TALK

Professor Kenosha Trent is sitting behind her large mahogany desk, wigless, in a formal navy blue suit. Behind her, through a large window, I can see a wet walkway meandering around trees below, and there's a light drizzle. She's not alone. In one of two black leather chairs across from her is an elderly woman with long white hair, a gray sweater, and jeans. It's the woman I saw sitting by her in our living room after my wandering, but at my house she was in a weird shimmering blue cloak.

"Hi, Cadence," Kenosha says. "We need to talk."

"Is this regarding school or witchcraft, Dr. Trent?" I ask, standing by the door. "If it's witchcraft, I'd rather not. I'm very busy."

"Is there a difference in Hawthorne?"

I grunt.

"You know, I'm surprised," Kenosha says. "I'm learning that you and Alondra are similar, Cadence. Not outwardly, you can be shy, but you two lecture similarly. Unless that wasn't you talking this morning? Was Alondra possessing you in class?"

"She never liked you. Allie simply respected your witchcraft."

"*Allie*? Who told you I used to refer to Alondra as *Allie*?" She squints at me, examining me. The old woman sitting beside me scrutinizes me too. "Your talk was good. I'd have preferred it without the personal hostility, but it was exemplary. I actually did want to join in the conversation, but just not when you asked publicly. Any talk about evil is evil. It is precisely why I was brought to teach here at Hawthorne University. Although evil's mystery can be entertaining, evil is as plain as day. Only evil people disguise bad behavior by questioning it. That's what Alondra used to do. But I'm not even convinced that it was you lecturing this morning. Was it you?"

"It was my lecture. It was a metaphysical lecture regarding symbols and how evil is perceived in the mind."

"But *Allie* showed up inside you at Jane Taylor's house, didn't she? Maddie's house? When Bryce told me, I immediately summoned Agnes."

Agnes nods and touches my hand with a shaky wrinkled hand. She smiles the sweetest smile. "Willow sent me to help you, dear," the old woman says in a British accent.

"Sit down, Cadence," Kenosha says.

I didn't even realize I had gotten up.

"Whether or not your teacher haunted you this morning," Agnes says, "she did possess you the night of your recent wandering, yes?"

"It is our belief," Kenosha says, "that an Ekimmu inside you was created by evil witchcraft by the Samhain Witch. She casted against you before, on Halloween, and confused you. She used Alondra to bring you to her lair. Now she's using her demon again."

"There's no demon inside me. I let Alondra's spirit reside there."

Agnes squints her bright sapphire eyes at me and then says, "You need our help."

"You're still seeing visions of the Samhain Witch?" asks Kenosha.

"I told you, I don't want to talk about witchcraft. I have a research project to prepare. *Your* research project, Dr. Trent."

"Cadence, if you say the lecture was by you, fine, I know you're smart enough. But Bryce and I also talked about how you have stage fright. You acted not only confident, but overconfident. That reminded me of Alondra. I also heard from Bryce that you saw the Samhain Witch during your recent wandering. It's March, Cadence. Melanie has never casted outside of Halloween. We are not meeting only over your possession, we're also here to discuss the Samhain Witch."

"How do you even know I saw the Samhain Witch? Kenosha, I appreciate that you're dean and I get that you want Bryce and I to revive Alondra's class, I love doing that, but you need to mind your own business."

"*Why do you think I'm here, Cadence!*" Kenosha snaps. She runs her hand over her face. "Will you please SIT down!"

No. I won't.

"Whether you like me or not, your teacher trusted me with you," says Kenosha. "She knew you'd have power and wouldn't know how to wield it."

"Be gentle, Willow," urges Agnes.

"If anyone gave the Samhain Witch power," I reply, "it's you after you cursed her grounds."

Kenosha's eyes bulge.

"Crescent Witch," Agnes warns Kenosha. "Love, Willow. Love. Love is the only way to fight this curse."

"Love, Andromeda?" Kenosha's nostrils are flaring. "Love? I loved Alondra, Cadence. You're wrong. I will not watch the terrible things that happened to her, happen to you. Yes, I did bad things. My magic contributed to those cursed grounds. I admitted it to you. That was evil, Cadence. Do you think I want the same evil to befall you?"

"You don't think I did my own lecture?"

"It seems that doubt resides in you as well," Agnes suggests with a smirk.

"Alondra knew your power," Kenosha says. "But she also knew that she was too sick to guide you. I told you that her curiosity about black magic destroyed her. I can help you remain a white witch, but if you're asking what evil is, Cadence..." She heaves a sigh. "Or experimenting with gray magic, black magic, or even sex magic—"

"*You know my thoughts on sex magic!*" I snap. I surprise myself by how pissed I sound. "*I never agreed to join my coven! I wouldn't have joined if I had known what they did to my best friend!*"

I mean, *fuck!* You want to fight, Kenosha? I nearly killed Alondra over her sex cult!

"This is not the way to move forward, Willow," Agnes says, shaking her head.

"Then tell me why you're lecturing like her?" Kenosha asks, leaning back in her chair. "Why are you tempting the dark arts? What do you think is the next step after you ask what evil is? Curiosity is one of evil's greatest temptations. The best way to deal with evil is to turn your back on it."

"*Like Bryce and Mira turned their backs on it!*" I shout. "Like all the other witches in my coven who ignored it! They all turned their backs on me by not telling me what was happening to Maddie. After she was *raped!* Alondra heard a mouthful when she was alive. I never forgave her and never will."

"Cadence," Agnes says gently, "you were prophesied to bring harmony. The rightward path. Love. That is why you are here in Hawthorne. That is why Kenosha is here in Hawthorne. We are not trying to change you. We are trying to help you retain who you are."

"You always reveal too much, Andromeda," Kenosha says, folding her arms.

"Gnosis leads to light," Agnes objects, raising a finger. "I agree with Cadence about secrecy. Secrecy is evil. But don't you see, child? You're angry about Kenosha mentioning what happened to your friends, but we are concerned about how you helped Alondra before she died. *You* brought Alondra out of her curse. *You* showed her the right path before she passed to the Summerland. She stopped backward practices of sex magic when she saw how it affected you. For *you*. And Kenosha left the leadership of her own coven in New Orleans, something no witch ever wants to do, under the promise of what was foreseen about you."

"How could Kenosha have known about me when she first came to Hawthorne?" I ask. "I remember seeing her at Beltane before I even knew anything about witchcraft. Did Alondra predict my witchcraft?"

"No," Agnes says. "Liam did."

"Agnes, that's enough!" Kenosha shakes her head.

"We fight the same enemy," Agnes says, losing her mirth. She suddenly looks grave. "I believe our enemy is not evil witches, but ourselves. Not by intent, but because our power makes us dangerous. I respect your words, Cadence. I believe you believe what you say, but I see confusion. You're young and ripe for being misdirected. Just as, after Halloween, Melanie trapped you into believing that you saw Alondra's spirit, she tricks you now by possessing you with a demon."

"I never even wanted to be a witch, Agnes."

"This is fortunate. It will maintain balance."

"I also cleaned my coven."

"Yes, you did," Agnes says. "But I hear you asked about evil in your lecture. Let me ask you what would happen if the Samhain Witch hurt your husband? Or your best friend, Madison? Or your brother? You have the power of the moon on your shoulders. What would you do with such power if you learned that it can be multiplied by your rage?"

It's quiet. Kenosha's avoiding my gaze, still pissed at me.

Well, I'm pissed at her too. The forest is lovely outside, the light flickering through the trees.

When I turn back to Agnes, she's just smiling. And that makes the office feel warmer and more comforting. Wait...is Agnes casting some sort of calming spell on me?

"I knew Alondra's mother," Agnes continues. "She was a close friend. A descendant of Abigail. Alondra too would never have believed that she became a witch by the turning of the wheel. Like you, she would claim that circumstances had made her into what she had become by her own will. And, like you when she was your age, she would have denied evil. But she turned evil around your age. So did her husband."

"Your heritage made you a witch, Cadence," says Kenosha with a nod. "Escoba for you, Abigail for Alondra." She lowers her head for a moment. She rubs her eyes. "Cadence, Alondra drew you here to Hawthorne. She researched and found you. When she discovered that you were growing up in Atlanta and applying—"

"She never contacted me. I applied on my own."

They fall silent. Then I feel stupid. Of course, they're implying Alondra used magic to bring me here.

"The council accepts your gnosis," Agnes says. "So must you, Kenosha. Now perhaps the council can persuade you, Cadence. You see, child, there are very few things we control. All of us follow the wheel of life, even those who do not practice witchcraft, hence the power of clairvoyance and prophecy." Agnes leans over and squeezes my hand. "Cadence, dear, I have just met you. You are kind. You are good. And we are so hopeful that you can help the witch council and our sisters, but I do not think you see our struggle clearly. Part of you is loyal to your former teacher, but she manipulated you when you lost your mother. Alondra used you."

"She did the same to her husband," Kenosha adds with a

nod. "She even turned Enora. Alondra is evil, Cadence. Why don't you accept this?"

"Alondra was one of the best people I ever knew!"

I'm so mad. I could never be angry at this sweet old woman sitting next to me, but Kenosha? The bitch who's sucking all the energy out of my husband like some leech or vampire?

"Alondra wasn't perfect, but she was human," I say. "She cared about me and my friends. She loved us. You claim that she manipulated me? How do I know that you and your council aren't manipulating me right now?"

"Sit down, Cadence!" Kenosha says, jumping up. *"We're not finished!"*

All the lights in her office shut off. A white fog rushes in around the tree trunks outside her window, as if smoke were gathering. Both witches stare out the window. Then they turn to me.

"Cadence," Kenosha says, looking up at the lights on the ceiling. "Please." She extends open palms and closes her eyes for a moment. The lights switch back on. "This is what we're talking about. This is why your teacher sent me here."

"Then why are you attacking her! Who's evil? You're the one who destroyed Melanie's family! You destroyed her life!"

"Alondra is evil, Cadence. You ask your students what evil is, look at your former teacher. You helped her before she died, but she still passed away in sin. Now you're being tested. The Samhain Witch is channeling all that negative energy because you're the new High Priestess of Hawthorne. She will use you to hurt all of us if you can't control it. Last year, I could protect us from Melanie with the remnants of your teacher's magic. Now this devil witch is using a demon inside you to invade your hallowed ground. The beast has devoted her entire life to hunting witches. With Alondra having passed, you need my help now."

But it starts pouring outside. There's thunder and wind

shakes the window. Then flashes of lightning. Agnes closes her eyes and looks down, nodding about something in contemplation. Kenosha just narrows hers, looking ready to leap over her desk and slap me.

"Alondra didn't lecture this morning?" Kenosha asks quietly. "Hmm, *Allie*? Did Allie decide on the lesson plan?"

"*No!*"

"Are you investigating black magic in your circle? Are you dabbling in mandrake? Nightshade? Henbane? Tell the council. The headmaster is here, Alondra. The more you delve into darkness, Cadence, the more you will turn dark, like your teacher, and the more you will keep secrets, until one day perhaps you, too, will practice sacrifice and *sex magic*."

The whole office starts shaking. A frame and a couple books fall from Kenosha's bookcase. And the lamps lighting the walkways outside, now turned on due to the heavy fog, are swaying. Is this an earthquake? I grab the arm of my chair to steady myself. But I'm still staring at Kenosha, wanting to tear her apart. Agnes oddly keeps dipping her head down, staring at the floor.

"Calm yourself, *white* witch," Kenosha warns, raising a finger.

"*Old prig!*" I shake, not from anger but fear. These words are Alondra's voice. "Accuse me of scheming? All you ever did your whole life, Kenosha, is scheme! Behold before you ALONDRA. You abandoned me when I needed you the most! I erred because I worked alone. I warn you two. Stand aside from this vessel. My Windstorm has more magic in a single finger than every witch's hand in your whole fucking feeble council!"

"Spoken with Luciferian pride, *Allie*," says Kenosha. She turns to Agnes. "Do you see her eyes! They're green, sister. Do you see! Do you now witness her possession, headmaster?"

"Stand down, Willow," Agnes says with a nod. But she doesn't look up. She's still nodding her head with her eyes closed. "I sense great power here. One is Windstorm, the other is from this demon."

"*There is no demon inside me!*" I shout. Thankfully, it's my own voice again. "*I allow Alondra's ghost to reside here!*"

Agnes finally looks up. "Do you want her inside you?"

I feel weak when I meet her gaze. I think this witch is casting some sort of calming spell again. She feels so soothing.

"You two can't help me," I reply quietly, shaking my head. "I'm sorry. But I think I know who can."

Bring him. Enough of them! Bring me my warlock.

"Who is the demon asking you to bring?" Agnes asks.

"Alondra is not a demon."

"But who is she asking for?" Agnes asks again. "Anyone named is in danger, Windstorm."

"Liam. Only Lee can help us."

"Liam won't help you, Cadence!" Kenosha objects, shaking her head, intensely exasperated. "Liam won't come anywhere near Hawthorne."

"Liam has sworn to never cast magic again," Agnes says. "His magic nearly destroyed him."

"Alondra's telling me to go see him and bring him back here," I say. "I don't know why, but I think it's the only way to stop the Samhain Witch and end this."

"Like what she told you about the Samhain Witch on Samhain, Cadence?" asks Kenosha. "Are you going to go hunt for Liam because this spirit inside you, your so-called teacher, just says so? We were trapped and almost killed when you listened to this spirit last time. You want to be trapped again? Do you see how stubborn she is, Andromeda?"

"Let her go," Agnes says, shaking her head. "She needs to see for herself. The council accepts."

"What if Melanie wants him there, High Priestess?" asks Kenosha. "Shouldn't we exorcise the Ekimmu first?"

"Liam won't return," Agnes says. "The only way to exorcise

this demon from Windstorm is if she is willing to let the demon leave her body." She turns to me. "I shall wait here for your return, but whether the spirit is a demon or actually her ghost, Alondra's spirit must be removed. Don't you at least agree to that, child?"

"You don't see danger in her leaving Hawthorne?" Kenosha asks.

"No, I see danger in her staying," Agnes says. Then she actually chuckles. "If Cadence is to help us, it cannot be by force. But, Windstorm, will you allow your sisters to gather this Friday sabbath to discuss the Samhain Witch and the exorcism of your possession after you return?"

"Yes."

"The council accepts," says Agnes.

Then we all just stare at each other. The storm has quieted, and there is only a light drizzle outside. And no more earthquake. I realize this meeting, or whatever the fuck these witches call it, is over. Since Agnes and their "council," whatever the hell a *council* is, "accept."

I wave to Agnes and leave, but I make sure to turn my back on Kenosha. If she weren't my dean, I tell you, I'd flip her off.

An office manager in a button-down and slacks rushes down the hallway. "Did you feel that earthquake, Ms. Wallace? That was so weird. I haven't felt a quake here in years. Are you all right?"

Maybe I didn't do enough? Maybe I should have had Kenosha's office completely cave in?

8

JUST NEED SOME INFO, DAD

"Mr. Hanley?"

I'm so relieved he finally picked up. But my hand is shaking holding my cellphone.

It's raining. I'm meandering down the walkway between the trees I was staring at through Kenosha's window. I wonder if those freak old ladies are staring down at me from the history building.

I'm so worked up. Those two old hags want to help me? They think you're a demon, Alondra. Can you believe that? They think you're evil. I mean...you kind of are.

"Cadence, is that you?" asks Uncle Hanley. As always, he sounds joyous as hell with his thick southern accent. "Why, Cadence Wallace, I'm so glad to hear ya. How the hell are you?"

"I'm fine, Uncle Hanley." *I'm really not, but, anyway.* "I need that address. Remember who we were talking about? Liam. I keep trying Liam's phone number, but he won't pick up. I'm talking about Liam Johansen, Alondra's first husband. I need his home address. I tried his number a million times, but he won't pick up. He won't answer texts or emails either. You said you have his house address too, right?"

"Yeah, I've got it. You going up to New York City?" And he laughs.

"Yeah."

He stops laughing.

But then we fall silent. Because how the hell am I going to explain any more of what's been happening? Uncle Hanley has no idea the *real* witchcraft his daughter was involved with. God, I wish I had the ability to channel Alondra whenever I want. Then I could fly to New York, and she could just lead me to Liam's house.

"I have to talk to Liam about...your daughter. There's some real important stuff I found at the house. If I can't reach him by phone or email, I'll have to just show up and hand it to him."

It's raining harder. Fortunately, I made it to a metal awning spanning a pathway between buildings. A kid rushes by, nearly colliding with me, on a skateboard. It's also crowded. Actually, it seems more crowded than usual, especially in the sudden downpour. Why?

I pass our library. That answers it. There are like a hundred students standing outside in front of the building. I remember my temper tantrum. They must have evacuated the building due to the earthquake.

Then it starts pouring harder. I realize Uncle Hanley is talking, but it's hard to hear him with the rain splattering against the metal ceiling.

"Sorry, can you hear me, Uncle Hanley? It's raining so hard."

"Yes, it's raining here too now. Yeah, I hear ya."

"There's stuff I found in your house that belongs to him. It's...some really important stuff, like bonds and things. I'd like to get it back to him."

"Cadence, I don't even know if Liam knows Alondra passed. I tried to call him before the funeral, and I got nothing. I'm sure he would have come otherwise. I've given up. Y'all know there was a lot of trouble between the two of them. For all I know, he doesn't even live there anymore."

"I know, but I have to try. It's that important."

"Okay. I'll send you what I got."

"Great. Thanks so much, Uncle Hanley."

"Sure. Look, I haven't come down to the house in a while. You and Bryce want to entertain an old fart?"

"The house is yours, Uncle Hanley," I say with a laugh. "We'd love to have you."

"In a few weeks, all right? I'll text you a date and you can let your lesser half know. It's your house by the way, not mine, Cadence."

"Okay, Uncle Hanley," I say with a chuckle.

"Take care of yourself. Good to hear ya. Hope to see you soon."

"Bye."

"Oh, if you get in touch with Liam, say hi for me. I miss that boy."

"Sure. Oh—" I dodge another student rushing by. "Daddy, I just want to thank you. You've always been there for me. I never really got to tell you that before. I really love you."

There's silence on the line. Did he hang up?

Oops! I realize my voice sounded like Alondra's and those last words were uttered by her voice. That's so weird! Not to mention I called him "*Daddy*."

"Bye," he finally says. "Love ya too, Cadence. Take care of yourself, hear? I hope to see you and Bryce soon."

9

———

JERSEY

"I HATE FLYING."

I'm standing beside Madison with our luggage as we wait by the drop off at the Newark airport parking lot. I'm clutching my arms tightly in a long thick coat. She's wearing a matching black newsboy cap. Our dark makeup is discreet and not too witchy. The curb is wet and it's foggy—it probably rained earlier.

"I mean, why does everyone agree to being packed like sardines, Maddie? And for all that money? It's like one giant elevator where no one says a word, but they're all right up your nose."

"I love it," Maddie finally says with a shrug. "It's so fun being up in the clouds. Hey, Katesy, why are we taking an Uber? Why not get in one of those classic yellow New York cabs?"

"I have the app."

A bunch of people are waiting outside near us. It was like this after Bryce dropped us off at the airport in Atlanta too. It's a bit unnerving being around so many people, coming from a small town.

"There's so many people."

"Not here, silly," Maddie says with a laugh. "This is just the airport. Wait till we get downtown. Are we really staying in Manhattan? Why? You said Liam's in New Jersey."

"I know what you want, Madison," I say, rolling my eyes.

"I love you so much," she says, clutching me tightly and giggling. "I'm so excited."

"That's why I wanted you to come."

Because I love her excitement. I really do. It's contagious. Unlike me, she loves traveling. I'm a homebody, happy to be alone in the forest.

"A hotel in Times Square, huh?" she asks. "Wow, can't wait to see all the lights. Maybe we'll get a view from the room. Times Square is close to Broadway, you know. I looked it up. Maybe we can see a show? What do you think? You want to do that?"

"Tomorrow we're heading to Jersey."

"Damien wanted to go too. It was too last minute. I'm sure your gorgeous professor did too. But my principal didn't care much. You know I'm the only one who doesn't have a steady job substitute teaching."

"I know."

"Hey." She hits me on the shoulder. Then she frowns. "I'm just glad I came to watch over you. I'm so worried about you. I think the one thing I needed last year was to be open about what was happening to me when Enora had me under her spell. You need to tell us so we can help you through whatever's going on, when you're cursed. That's why I thought, though looney, that this was a good idea."

"It's not a curse. I told you everything, Maddie."

"Sure."

"Does your mom forgive me?"

"She loves you, Cadence," Maddie says with a nod. "You could never upset her."

My cellphone buzzes in my purse. It's Bryce.

"You guys safe?"

"Aha. We're fine, Bryce. We just touched down."

"Miss you."

"You dropped us off three hours ago," I reply with a laugh.

"Yeah, but I still miss you. Okay, when you get into the hotel at Times Square, can you call me?"

"Sure, Bryce."

"Love you."

"Love you too."

I stuff my phone back in my bag. Maddie's staring out at all the cars rushing by with a big smirk. I bet she's daydreaming about a Broadway show or something.

"Your brother doesn't call me every minute like that," she says.

"Honestly, it's kind of annoying. Bryce has been crazy ever since your mom's house. He's always worried about me. Like he's looking over our future family or something."

"Are you pregnant, Cadence?"

"Of course not, stupid!" I say, laughing. People turn, staring at us. "Shut up."

"You know, I've been thinking, Alondra almost killed you last Halloween asking you to go to Alabama. You know, you were almost strangled to death. Even Enora was nearly killed. That was all that voice in your head was doing. So, are we going to be killed here too?"

"I keep telling everybody, it's really Alondra inside me. No one believes me, but you saw her at your mom's house. How could some demon know all that stuff about your mom? I trust her." Then I point at a van pulling up to the curb. "He's here."

The drive is nice. Actually, just sitting in a roomy seat versus a sardine can is nice. I can spread out my legs and lean back and just gaze out at the fields around Newark. Or just close my eyes. Why am I always sleepy when traveling?

"Hey look, Katie! Look!" She pulls out her phone and starts taking pictures. "It's so pretty. Look, babe!"

The first glimpse of the New York skyline in the distance is making Maddie go bonkers. It's all she can do to not throw the door open and jump out of the car. The sky is clear enough to show the skyscrapers across the water, even though the horizon is tinged orange.

"Hey, is that the Freedom Tower, Cadence? That big building up there? Holy shit! Is it?" She leans forward, tapping the driver's shoulder and pointing. "Sir? Sir, is that the Freedom Tower?"

Our short, thin older driver is wearing glasses. He just stares at the road.

"New York," Maddie whispers in my ear, cupping her mouth. Then she says to me, more quietly, "Can we go up one of those buildings, Katesy? Please? I've never been up a skyscraper before."

"I don't know if we'll have time."

"Well, at least the Empire State Building. Frida told me they have a statue of King Kong and lots of cool monitors simulating the big ape attacking people from the movie. She said the lookout is so much fun. And she said there's this really tall building where you can stand on glass and look way down, hundreds of feet, through a window. It's called the..." She puts her finger to her cheek. "The Summit. We should go tomorrow. What do you think? Unless you're afraid of heights. Or we could just rent bikes in Central Park. Maybe in the early morning, huh, babe? If you need to head back to New Jersey, we can see Liam later in the afternoon?"

"It's going to take a lot of our time just traveling to Liam's. But I really don't even know if Liam will be there."

"Kinda hope he isn't," she says with a big grimace, staring outside again. "Sorry."

"I'm just happy you came, Madds," I say, patting her hand.

She leans over and embraces me. "Anything for my bestie. I'm so excited! New York. What a fabulous idea."

The drive from New York City into New Jersey takes much longer than anticipated. It's sort of sucked all of yesterday's energy out of Madison. That's how bad the traffic is. She won't tell me, she just keeps flashing a grin, but I think we've been in the cab for over two hours. She told me she wanted to go to the Museum of Modern Art to check out Dali and Magritte. Doesn't look like we're going to have time now.

You know, Bryce would have loved seeing Magritte's paintings in the museum. Bryce taught us about a painting featured there in our art history class a few years ago: *The Lovers*. He thought he was being clever because we were in a fight and the painting has two lovers in white shrouds.

It seems like we've been on the road forever. Liam must live really far from Manhattan. First there was traffic, then, after driving through that long underground tunnel again, we still had to drive through suburbs. The taxi driver in our yellow cab is a dark-skinned lady with braided hair, and she's completely silent. Of course, Maddie tried to talk to her. We chose a yellow car this time because Maddie wanted to be in a yellow taxi.

"If this takes too long, you should return to the hotel."

"Are you kidding? I'm here for you, Kates."

"No, if we're running behind, just take a cab back to the hotel. I'll meet you tonight. I don't want to mess up your trip."

"The museum needs reservations, dope. Forget it. I didn't come here for New York City, I came here for you."

But she doesn't seem very happy saying that.

A drop of water trickles down the passenger window in front of a zillion narrow two- to three-floor buildings rushing by. The architecture here is neat. They're all these tall, narrow stacked homes.

Maddie grunts as we enter another highway. But we quickly exit on an off-ramp, pass a gas station, and then turn into a narrow suburban street. It's full of more of these stacked narrow houses in rows.

Then the driver finally stops by a curb.

Are we here? Who can tell? The homes don't look much different from neighborhoods we've passed over the last half an hour.

I check the numbers over a garage. According to Uncle Hanley, this is the right address.

We get out and stand before a small white house with wood siding and a dark gray roof. The wood porch over the garage is distinctive. It has white wooden columns and reminds me a little of my house, Alondra's house, back home in Hawthorne.

We walk up and my friend rings the doorbell. Then she grumbles because no one answers. I jump when Maddie raps harder with her fist. The door cracks open, and a middle-aged woman with glasses and blond hair greets us.

"Yes?" she asks with a Jersey accent and smile. "Can I help you?"

"We're looking for Liam," Maddie answers. "Liam Johansen."

The woman furrows her brow. Then she nods slowly, looking behind her. "Lee, someone's here to see you."

I sigh deeply in relief. Now I don't have to worry anymore about being murdered by my friend.

Inside is a warm home. I don't mean physically warm; I mean it feels inviting. There are wood floors with two matching brown leather couches and white swivel chairs. A large wooden cross is on a wall near the chimney, and the bookcase is full of more indoor plants than books. There are a few really large plants, too, almost like small trees. And everything smells nice. I think it's scented incense or candles. Cinnamon.

A toddler with long golden-blond hair runs by us. She waves her hand as if it's an afterthought then runs upstairs.

I spot Liam while we're still at the threshold. He's in a white T-shirt and gray sweatpants, and he's got thin red-gray hair and a beard. I don't recall seeing him with thick facial hair. I also don't recall seeing any gray hair. Did he have gray hair on Beltane? I can't remember. He's always so young in my visions.

"I'm Cadence," I say to him, with a tone as if to say *you know who I am.* But does he remember? "This is my friend, Madison. Maddie Taylor. Jane Taylor's daughter."

"I know," he says with a nod.

"Oh, you know these girls?" asks the blond woman. Then she smiles at us and says, "Well, you're welcome to come in then."

"I knew their mothers," Liam says.

"Well, you didn't know my mother," I correct him with a chuckle, touching my chest. "But Maddie's mom, Aunt Jane, was a good friend of yours, right?"

"Your mother was Alondra."

What? What the hell is that supposed to mean?

The woman gives Liam a really funny look. Then she heads down a hallway.

Maddie and I sit together on a brown leather couch. Liam doesn't sit. He stands with his hands in his pockets, staring at us uncomfortably.

"You two want tea?" the woman hollers from the kitchen.

"Yes, please," Maddie replies.

Then the oddest thing happens. Liam turns around and heads down the hallway, leaving Maddie and me alone.

"Come on, Sophie, let's play ball," I hear him say down the hall.

I hear clapping and then see the little tyke rush down the stairs again. The back door opens. Then it slams shut.

Madison takes her newsboy cap off and looks at me lifting an eyebrow, totally bewildered. Then she mouths *"what the fuck?"*

"I'm Pamela," the woman says, bringing over a tray with four white porcelain cups. She puts it down on a mahogany table beside us. "Forgive me, but the water's microwaved. Stove isn't working, but at least it's quick, right?" She smiles. Pamela seems nice. "Jane was such a good friend. Liam tells me stories about her all the time when he talks about college. She's your mom, huh?"

Madison nods.

"His college years meant so much to him," Pamela says. "But..." She hesitates for a moment and looks down the hall. "He's tried to forget about all of it too. It was a traumatic time. If you knew my husband, you'd know that he's the nicest man in the world."

That's what Aunt Jane said. But the nicest man in the world just escaped to go play ball with a little girl after we traveled a thousand miles.

I grab a cup of tea. It's good. Earl Gray. But I catch my hand shaking as I hold the porcelain cup. I'm pretty worked up. For days, I've been wanting to meet Liam. I've been completely obsessed, and I'm so hoping he can help me. But, what if I'm wrong?

I hear that little girl laughing outside.

"Are you just visiting or do you two live around here?" Pamela asks.

"We're traveling from Hawthorne," Maddie says. "Hawthorne is near Atlanta. Cadence over here teaches history at the college."

"I'm a graduate student," I say with a nod.

"The university Liam went to," Pamela says. "Do you go to school there too?"

"Just graduated," Maddie says. "I have a job substitute teaching at a high school in Flintwood. Flintwood's a town near Hawthorne. And..." She puts her arm around me. "Katie and I are besties."

"I see you two dress alike," Pamela says with a nod and a chuckle.

I take my cap off and run my fingers through my long dark hair. She's right about that. We're wearing matching black T-shirts and pants and black lipstick (sans our witchy eyeliner) and are wearing our dark hair long.

I look down the hallway again.

"What brings you two to New Jersey?"

I find myself getting up. Pamela doesn't stop me; she just turns to Maddie and sips more tea, waiting for her response. As my friend replies, I mosey down the hallway.

It's then that it dawns on me that even the layout of the house is similar to Alondra's, or my, house. I even pass a dining room to my left. There's no grand window looking out onto the forest, there's no window at all, but the room's position is the same.

But all similarities end when I see the backyard. Outside is a very small square yard made of concrete, with a barbecue, surrounded by the neighbors' houses. Liam is carefully throwing a tennis ball to the little girl. She seems barely old enough to catch, because the ball is about the size of her palm.

"I'm sorry, Lee," I say, stepping outside.

Liam stops throwing. He quickly shakes his head. He's spooked because my voice sounded like Alondra's. I'm spooked too.

"Don't do that," he says angrily with his back still turned. "Don't use her voice."

"Are you okay, Daddy?" asks the little girl.

He picks up the ball and crouches down, gesturing to her that he's going to throw it again. "Okay, now pay attention and try to catch it, Sophie. Okay? You can do it."

And he throws the ball to Sophie. She misses the ball, trying to catch it with both hands. And all the while I'm standing over them feeling stupid.

"Is she okay, Daddy?" asks the little girl, pointing up at me.

"Alondra asked me to see you." Thankfully, it's my voice again. "That's why I came."

"I can't help you. I'm not a witch anymore."

"I didn't know where else to turn."

"Did you ask Kenosha?"

"Yes. She even brought another witch. They both think Alondra's possessing me. But this isn't some Ekimmu or demon. Alondra's ghost is actually inside me. It's your wife. I'm afraid Alondra never passed to the Summerland, Mr. Johansen. I have some control of her, but sometimes, like a second ago, I don't. And Kenosha and Agnes don't know how to help me. So I came here. I don't know what else to do. Your wife is really inside me and she's desperate, for some reason, for you to return to Hawthorne."

"Agnes visited you?" he asks, finally turning and looking up at me. "Andromeda?"

"Yes, but they can't help," I reply with a nod.

"They never could," he says with the hint of a grin. "They never really had any more magic than Allie and I did. But Kenosha's moved there for you." He stands up and runs his hand over the little girl's messy golden hair. "Sophie, go play in your room, okay? We can throw the ball together later."

"Okay, Daddy." The little girl looks up at me and says, "Bye, bye."

Then Liam faces me. He has nice eyes, dark and intelligent, like Bryce's.

"Blessed be, Windstorm." He gets up and shakes my hand.

But that sounded sarcastic. Then he adds, calmly, "We arranged for Kenosha to help you. Why hasn't Willow helped?"

"She's trying. She wants to meet with the coven on Friday. But she doesn't even understand what's going on."

I stroke his fingers, still in my hand, after I feel his strong grip. Then I look up into his eyes again, smiling seductively. He's cute. I have an urge to take him in my arms and...

He yanks his hand back.

"Allie gave you the book," he says quickly. "She arranged everything to help you in her absence, including bringing in Willow."

"Kenosha says that Alondra manipulated me. She claims she schemed to bring me to Hawthorne. I never wanted to be a witch. And my former teacher, your wife, although a major pain in the butt, always seemed to know what was going on. I don't. But Kenosha doesn't have a clue. No one does now."

"Alondra was always a pain in the ass," he says with a laugh. "She manipulated everything and everyone, even those she loved. She couldn't help it. But I loved her. And I bet you did too."

I nod and we laugh.

"But why'd you come all the way here, Cadence?"

"Someone doesn't answer their phone."

"I answer it," he says running his hand through his thinning hair. "Just not any number with Hawthorne's area code. Sorry. God, it must be so difficult for you to have come this far."

"Alondra's asking you to return with me to Hawthorne. She's obsessed. I don't know why. Just like she needs Aunt Jane's help too. She pesters me constantly, making me write your name in my Book of Shadows, *Broomstick*. Her ghost even materialized in front of me in our coffee house asking why I hadn't brought you back yet."

"I didn't even attend her funeral, Cadence. I get how important this must be to you, but you must know I can never go back there."

"Four months ago, I went to Winona's house. You know, the house in Geneva Forest, Alabama?" I talk quickly because I feel like I've been wanting to get all this stuff off my mind for weeks. Or maybe it's because I'm worried he's going to walk away again? "I didn't see Winona at that house, I saw her sister, Melanie. Melanie's changed. She's become something inhuman. A monster. It's since then that Alondra started appearing. Not just appearing as a ghost wandering my school, like I saw last year, but *possessing* me. I had a huge fight with Aunt Jane, Maddie's mom. But it wasn't me, it was Alondra. Apparently, Alondra and Jane were close. I didn't even know Maddie's mom knew Alondra until we fought."

"Alondra and Jane were best friends."

"Yes. But Aunt Jane had been mum about that ever since I met Maddie in my freshman year. And Jane was as thrilled about seeing Alondra inside me as you were. Anyway, after I fought Maddie's mom, or Alondra did, I went on a witch wandering. I saw the Samhain Witch in a trance. She casted an evil curse. But before... I..."

Okay, look, I'm not going to tell him about having sex with him. That was so fucking weird!

"I... I saw you and Allie inside my living room. Alondra's spirit keeps showing me the past. Kenosha thinks the Samhain Witch is trying to harm me by tricking me. I don't think so. Ever since Halloween, Kenosha's thought that the Samhain Witch has tried to trick me, but I think Alondra's appeared to actually help Melanie."

"You can't help Melanie."

"Kenosha agrees with you there. But she's wrong about Alondra. She thinks Melanie is casting a demon possession in me that's impersonating your wife. I tell you, she's not. Alondra's spirit is pleasant inside me. I love her. But Alondra never passed into the Summerland, Mr. Johansen. I'm sorry to tell you this, it's horrible, but I think your wife is roaming this Earth as a ghost. Her spirit is not free, it resides inside me. But..." I shake my head. "That's not even all of it. She and I want to be together. It's like we have to be together in order to save Hawthorne."

Liam runs his hand through his hair again. Then he leans against the wall near the door and folds his arms. I glance at his hair. I've always loved that hair. Just like I love Bryce's—it's feathery and soft. What I would do right now to run my fingers—

"What can I do?"

"I get that Alondra sent Kenosha to help me, but she can't. Kenosha and the other witches don't understand how to fix the past."

"Agnes visited you?"

"Before I left," I say with a nod, "Agnes came to see me. Yes. To help me. They're trying to help me."

"Agnes is the leader of the council."

"What the hell is the council? Kenosha hinted at it, but she didn't tell me much."

"The witch council is a group of a hundred or more powerful witches throughout the world. They come together to share spell casting. They're omnipotent. Arrogant. Alondra was always a renegade. They really have no more power than she and I ever did, it's just that they work together. Rumor has it that they are involved with more things in our world than just witchcraft. But honestly, they're no more powerful than Alondra was, probably less so."

"Yes! I believe that. That's why I'm here! That's why you have to return to Hawthorne with me. Of course, I wouldn't have come all this way if you just answered your damn phone."

"God, I thought you were simply imitating her to get my attention," he says with a nod, more to himself. Then he scrutinizes my eyes. "Allie is *actually* inside there? In you? That's incredible."

"It's horrible," I say, covering my eyes. "I hate my eyes."

"Cadence, I don't practice the arts anymore. I see patients. I'm a psychologist. I don't dabble in the occult or the supernatural. What would you have me do? Don't you see, I loved my former wife, but I didn't even return to Hawthorne when Allie was dying."

"I'm so desperate."

"I can't. I'm sorry."

"Why?"

He shakes his head and looks down.

"The only thing that brought me back to Hawthorne over the years was you," he says. "I came back to hand Allie back her book. For you. That was it. To hand you your book."

"But Alondra is asking for you now. She never asked before, did she? There's something so vital, or something so horrible, happening back home that even the head witch of the council can't fix it. You have to return. I really think you're the only one who can help us."

"She'd never ask anything from anyone," he says with a nod and a smirk. "But she hinted at inviting me plenty of times. She wanted to see me again before she passed. We spoke and corresponded. Then we fought again. That was always how it was with us, Cadence."

"Her dad wasn't even sure you knew she passed away."

"Kenosha told me long after the funeral." He shrugs and smirks. "I knew she was sick, but I told you, I never answered calls. Only one day, for some reason, I picked up Kenosha's call."

"I don't know where else to turn. If you don't return to Hawthorne, you're not only hurting her, you're hurting me and my friends."

"I swore to never practice magic again, Cadence. No, I can't help you with witchcraft. I'm sorry."

"I'm not asking you to cast a spell. I just need you to—"

But then, apparently, he's had enough. He turns his back on me, opens the door, and finally does what I feared he'd do all along. He heads back into the house. But it's not done in anger. He walks slowly, almost pensively.

I follow.

When we approach the living room, Pamela gets up.

"Can I talk to you for a moment alone?" Pamela asks.

I plop back on the sofa near Maddie. Maddie whispers, a little too loud: "Well, can he help us or not?"

"Shh. No."

"No? Then...can we...*go?*"

Because she wants to go sightseeing. I get it. Maybe we should. But, although Pam and Liam are in the kitchen talking "alone," we have no difficulty hearing them. And that cheers Maddie up because eavesdropping, along with thievery, is among her favorite pastimes.

"Whatever's happening to these young girls, they need our help, Lee," Pam says. "Maddie told me that her friend is so desperate. They traveled so far just to see you. Can't you help them somehow?"

"I swore, Pam. I swore to never cast again. I can't."

"Isn't there something you can do? Can't you just show up and not practice magic?"

"Only witchcraft can help her. No more magic, Pam."

"Fine. But let them stay the night at least. There's no casting spells, no magic, in that, right?"

"Pam..." Liam sounds pained. It's almost cute.

"You called that girl Alondra's daughter," Pam says almost in a whisper. "That makes her *my* daughter, honey. Please, at least let *our* daughter stay the night."

Liam and Pamela return to the living room.

"We should probably go," Maddie says, getting up.

"It'll be dark in another half hour," Pamela says, shaking her head. "Just stay over. You two can take our guest room."

"Alondra was always welcome here," Liam says. "Please, Cadence, stay, it's not a bother. You're family. And your mom and I were really good friends in college, Madison. We'd love for you both to stay the night."

And that's when I see what Jane likes about Liam. He is nice, like Bryce. But a bit more edgy, like me. His kindness makes me wonder how he survived being married to that wicked witch Alondra. Wait...I guess he didn't. He left her. I guess the real wonder is how I stayed with Alondra.

"Daddy?" asks little Sophie, running down the stairs. "Play ball?"

"Our guests can play with you, sweetheart," Liam says with a smile. "If they'd like?"

"Thank you, Mr. Johansen," I say.

"Call me Lee."

10

TIMES SQUARE

Maddie's crouched over a curb scrutinizing a bunch of small leather purses on the ground. The guy selling them has on a large cap, a poncho, and sunglasses. The glasses are weird because it's the middle of the night. He's tried to sell me stuff too, but I keep looking away. My eyes fall on zillions of people passing by, and I have to keep repositioning myself near my friend so that people don't run into me. I'm also holding my small purse tightly under my arm because I don't want it swiped. It's just so busy.

Only twenty yards away a huge group of guys is breakdancing. They keep doing this show over and over again with tourists. I know because I saw all of them here the other night too.

I glance up at the huge bright screen-tower lighting the streets. There's honking. And some shouting. Yep, we're in Times Square in New York City not far from our hotel. And Maddie's loving it.

"Ooh, look at this one, Kates! This one's so cute." Maddie shows it to me. It's a small Louis Vuitton purse with LV symbols. She shows it off, slinging it on her shoulder. "Whatcha think?"

"I think it's hot. Or fake."

"Looks pretty hot to me." She lifts her purse, touching the fabric with her fingers. Then she winks at me with a large grin. "They're all hot, aren't they?" she says with a smile. She shrugs. "Hey, *I'm* not the one stealing this time."

"Twenty dollars," says the guy with shades.

I shake my head.

Maddie pulls a twenty dollar bill out of her purse and hands it to the weirdo.

"Come on," Maddie says, hooking her arm with mine. "We need a selfie together by the signs."

She rushes me into the street, and she's about a foot away from being splattered by a car. There's honking and Maddie's laughing like crazy. She runs a little farther down the sidewalk and she stops. Then she runs her fingers through her hair and through mine.

"Come on, Cadence! Let's take a selfie." And she embraces me tightly with the tower of signs behind us. "That's shit, Cadence! Come on. Smile real big. At least act like you're happy."

I force a smile.

"Bigger."

I try.

"Bigger." Then Maddie hugs me and laughs. "Isn't this fun? Come on, let's go shopping."

And I'm rushing to keep up with her.

She dashes into a room with a ton of small metal Statues of Liberty on a wood table, rows of baseball caps, another table of shot glasses, and refrigerator magnets posted on a board. You name it, this place has it. I see stairs so it's two to three stories too. And, of course, there are bodies bumping into one another.

As I stand behind Maddie as she's perusing, she asks, "What's the matter, Cadence?"

"Nothing."

"What do I keep telling you? No secrets, remember. Tell me what's on your mind."

"You know, Maddie, what's the matter. I was hoping Liam would be going with us back to Hawthorne."

"Somehow I knew he wouldn't. But that's okay. I've had so much fun on this trip with you."

"I'm glad."

"Hey, at least you're still faithful to Bryce," she says, cocking her head back. I hit her arm. "I thought you were worried about Bryce killing you for missing lecture."

"You wanted to see the museum."

"Wasn't it fabs? Bryce is so nice to let you leave on Monday. And we got him a poster of his favorite painting. You know, *The Lovers*."

"I lied and told him we needed to stay another day with Liam."

"Well, we did, but he wasn't willing to join us. Thanks, babe. I had so much fun." She's back to browsing, looking at a ton of T-shirts. She puts a few up against my chest. "Sucks we have to go back to trees. Hey, let's get Damie and your hubby a souvenir T-shirt to wear around the forest. You know, like that shirt John Lennon wore. Won't that just be funny as hell wearing a New York tourist shirt in Hawthorne Forest? We can wear it during one of our sabbath ceremonies."

"Thanks for coming, Maddie."

"Oh, Cadence," she says. Then she takes another T-shirt down and shows it to me. She shakes her head. "Cheer up. It was fun. Thank *you*. I'm getting a T-shirt for you, by the way, whether you say yes or no."

11

BLACK MIRROR

"*Lux alba*. Blessings come from Hecate. Glory be the stars. Let not a cloud block Selene. And if it be, let the rays of light come forth in the morrow. Blessed be our Hawthorne coven under our gods Gaia, Selene, and Astraeus. Blessed be. May all never thirst."

It's Friday. I'm with my sisters, and all the anxiety I felt all week has faded. I just always feel good with my circle, particularly when I say those words to my coven. Because these aren't just witches, these are my friends.

"May you never thirst, Windstorm," Kenosha replies with a nod. She's bald in her green cloak, but you can't tell right now because she has her hood over her head. That old witch Agnes is in glistening blue, sitting beside her. Agnes is smiling. She's always smiley.

"May you never thirst," my sisters echo. Then each of them turns to the person beside them, hugs them, and kisses their cheeks.

"I've brought a guest—"

"Cadence is officiating," Bryce interrupts Kenosha. Boy, he's really starting to hate Kenosha too.

"Of course, High Priest," Kenosha says, folding her arms and nodding.

I stand up and raise my arms. My sleeves fall from my wrists.

"As I draw down the moon," I say, "I take down the light from blessed Diana amidst the stars, revealing one soul, Atman, blessed within our circle. I ask us all to reflect on the love of our circle. *Lux alba*."

"*Lux alba*," says Bryce, closing his eyes.

"*Lux alba*," repeats everyone.

In the past, I might have let the flames of our bonfire rise. Not tonight. I feel more serenity than power. So I simply sit back down.

"There are two concerns I wish to bring to our circle tonight, sisters," I say. "You know I said before that those of us who went to Alabama don't like talking about what happened in Geneva Forest. You heard about the haunted house."

"I wish I could have been there," says Natasha with a grin.

"Me too," says Mandy next to her.

"I don't," Frida says. "From what Katie tells me, I'm glad Greg and I were away that night."

"You two had a date?" I ask with a smile.

Frida nods with a bigger grin.

"When are you two tying the knot, Frida?" asks Bryce.

"Bryce," I say, hitting his shoulder. "Come on. Leave her alone."

But he's right. She's been engaged long enough. Of course, as witches, tying the knot comes with a totally different meaning. Our weddings are literally *a knot*—we partake in handfasting marriage ceremonies.

"I don't mind," Frida says. "I don't mind if we never get married, guys. As long as we're together."

"That is so sweet, Frida," I say. "I love that."

"Yeah," Maddie says, "but...when are you two getting married?"

Everyone laughs.

Everyone except Kenosha. Across the bonfire, she's brooding. Not only did Bryce shush her, but everyone is interrupting her to talk about boys. This is what's fun about my coven. Like I said, we're not only witches, we're friends. Someone like Kenosha can't understand that. At least Agnes is still smiling.

"I think it's time, Frida," Bryce says, leaning back in his chair and straightening his black cloak.

"Let them take their time," I say with a chuckle. "Not everyone finds the perfect man like you, Bryce."

"You and your husband are very much in love," Agnes says to both of us. "I sense it. Your anahata binds this circle in love."

"Thank you, Agnes," I say with a nod. Hmm, perhaps the old lady isn't so bad.

"Soon, Bryce," Frida says. "He's just trying to get stuff together back home in New York. Speaking of New York, how was it for you and Maddie, Katie? Did you make it to Chelsea Market? High Line? I told you, that is our favorite place to shop."

"We didn't have time, Frida," I say. "We just hung around Times Square."

"It was so much fun, guys," Maddie chimes in. "I showed some of you the pics of Kates and me. We didn't just do Times Square. We made it up the Empire State Building, Windstorm, don't forget that. And their modern art museum. I saw Bryce's favorite painting, *The Lovers*."

"That's not my favorite painting," Bryce objects. "But it's a good one. I wish I could have seen it with you guys."

"We also checked out the Rockefeller Center. You know, where they ice skate in the movies and where they have that really big toy store and huge Christmas tree for Christmas."

"I liked the museum," I say. "The coolest thing there was

this three-dimensional painting by Dali. It was done with a few layers in 3-D. It wasn't a painting really, but it was so cool."

At this point, Kenosha looks ready to leap over the bonfire and smack Bryce and me on the head.

Okay. Fine.

"Guys, I want to introduce you all to two very important guests tonight," I say. "They are leaders of their covens, very powerful High Priestesses. Of course, we've had Willow in our circle before."

"Yatu, Windstorm," Kenosha says with a nod.

"But accompanying Willow is another very important guest. Agnes of her Selene coven. Her Selene coven in England is said to have been the first known Celtic coven in the world, maybe the first organized coven ever. Her name, under blessed Diana, is Andromeda."

"Yatu, witches," says Agnes.

"Yatu," say all my sisters.

"I yield the floor to Willow and Andromeda."

But then, before Kenosha can finally speak, my circle goes absolutely nuts. First Josie and Debra jump up. Then Frida cocks her head and jumps up too. I'm freaking out thinking I'm going to turn around and see a ghost or Enora. Firelight brightens over my shoulder. That's torchlight, I think.

"Mira!" cries Maddie.

A heavyset witch in a black cloak and long draping black dress, with her distinctive red and black demon tattoos and black makeup, is walking to us carrying a fiery torch.

"Tradition allows witches to visit their coven by invitation, High Priestess," Mira says formally. "May I join this ceremony, Windstorm?"

I answer by jumping up and throwing my arms around her.

"I take that as a yes," Mira says with a laugh.

Then she walks over and touches her torchlight to our bonfire.

"I've missed you so much," I say.

"Me too, Cadence," Mira says. But then she loses her smile and walks right up to me, examining my eyes. "I came to help. Courtney couldn't make it, but Maddie told me everything. We've been so worried about you."

And then our sabbath ceremony falls apart. All my friends leave their seats and start hugging Mira and kissing her cheeks.

After more hugging and yapping, Kenosha finally says, "Cadence, I'm happy to bring guests to your circle, yatu, Raven, but we really have to get on with the problem at hand."

"Well, we'll need an extra chair," I say.

"I'll get one," says Bryce.

"No, Bryce," Mira says. "I can sit comfortably on the grass before the fire. I just want to hear what Willow has to say."

And now there are sixteen of us around the fire. It's a clear, starry night and flickering light from our large bonfire casts shadows over the field. It's nice. Tranquil.

"I yield the floor to Willow," I say again, sitting down. But then I lean over Frida and whisper to Mira, "We'll talk later."

"I'm afraid this is the problem, witches," says Kenosha. "Cadence is dealing with a very serious problem. Distractions are only going to make her condition worse."

Well, now all my friends hate her as much as Bryce and I do. I hardly think our love for each other is a *distraction*. The problem with you, Kenosha, is that you've got a big stick up—

"Upon Samhain," Kenosha continues, "the Samhain Witch's power has grown more powerful than ever. You all heard what happened last Halloween. The beast used Windstorm's love for your previous teacher, Alondra, to trap her into thinking that she could save her family in Alabama. It was a trap. But the house there is more in ruins than an actual home. I'm not sure I would have had to warn Cadence if she knew there was barely even a house to haunt. But what I did know is that every year for the past two decades, Melanie, The Samhain Witch, has been casting evil against your coven. When Alondra was alive, she and I were able to cast protective spells. But with the recent passing of Falconsong, the Samhain Witch's power has grown. It was all I could do to rescue Cadence."

"Cadence rescued us," Bryce says, shaking his head. "She used her grimoire to cast a spell and keep Melanie trapped in her house."

"I distinctly remember Kenosha helping Cadence, Bryce," says Mira with a smile. Mira loves us, but she's hardly averse to fighting.

"Kenosha did help save me," I say with a nod. "If she hadn't come, I wouldn't have been able to cast that spell, and that witch probably would have killed me, Bryce. I owe Kenosha my life. It was both our powers that got us out."

"Thank you, Cadence," Kenosha says. "Well, since the event, I've seen something I haven't seen for decades. This magic, this evil, is now possessing your High Priestess. This is why I invited Agnes, blessed Andromeda, who has traveled so far. We need a shield spell to be cast within this circle. We're both here to ask if your coven is willing to prepare for this spell?"

"It is your coven, Windstorm," Agnes says. "Can we prepare this conjuring?"

"Yes. Only if the circle agrees. And only if they completely understand everything." I turn to Frida. Josie and Chandra are leaning forward, looking intently at me. The fire flickers over their faces, adorned with distinctive witchy black makeup. "You all need to know, though, that I disagree over my *so-called* problem. Alondra's spirit is residing inside me. She is not a demon. She's actually our teacher. Our teacher's ghost."

But that creeps everyone out even more. Except Mira. As always, Mira seems more excited than afraid. I have a feeling she didn't come only to help me, she wanted to see Alondra's spirit for herself.

"I went to New York to find Liam, guys," I continue. "Liam

Johansen, Alondra's first husband. I wanted him to return here because...I'm afraid Allie doesn't think any witch can help us except Liam. Allie's asking, inside of me, for Liam to return to Hawthorne."

"There you go saying *Allie*, Cadence," Kenosha says. "You've been claiming you have control over your possession, but you don't. Alondra didn't go by Allie when you went to college here."

"Liam still calls her Allie," I say.

"The Samhain Witch is casting an Ekimmu inside you," Kenosha says. "You think it's Alondra, but it isn't. Even the council believes this possession is evil."

"It is not a possession." I turn once again to my friends. "Guys, there's something else. You need to know what Kenosha told me on Halloween. The reason Melanie has so much power."

"Cadence," Kenosha objects, "some things I tell you in private are not meant to be made public."

"This is my circle. These are my friends. They need to know, Willow. It's only fair. I've told them countless times that we cannot keep secrets."

"The council agrees, Willow," Agnes says calmly, with a solemn nod. "Her circle needs to know. We spoke of gnosis and the importance of openness in these difficult times."

"Agnes," Kenosha says. "There are some things I am ashamed of."

Shame... Embarrassment...mortification. Hmm, that reminds me of the wandering I had. Embarrassment over my botched lecture had triggered me to be even more humiliated with Liam and the frog. I was completely humiliated by my sexual encounter with Liam, but I was far more mortified after discovering what I had been doing with myself and that filthy, disgusting frog in the mud. I was masturbating. That part was so gross that I couldn't even unveil it to my best friend. And I won't ever. I wonder if there is some connection between embarrassment and Melanie's power?

"The coven needs to know everything if they are to work together, Willow," says Agnes.

"I disagree," Kenosha says, "I think this knowledge of the past is defeating our cause."

"Sisters," I say. I straighten my cloak. Honestly, I don't really want to snitch on Kenosha either. "Many years ago, the two High Priestesses here used magic and fought against Alondra."

"Cadence!" snaps Kenosha.

"This is my coven."

Agnes closes her eyes and nods.

"Kenosha cast a spell against Alondra in Alabama cursing Melanie's—"

I'm interrupted by a thousand whispers. It's a mix of whispering and laughter, as if coming from an audience in a lecture hall. Then I hear a child's laughter pounding my ears. Then children screaming. The sounds seem to be bouncing off the trees in my backyard, as if the trunks and branches are amplifying the noise, but no one else seems to hear anything.

I cover my ears and head.

"Cadence?" asks Kenosha. "*Cadence!?*"

All my sisters are looking at me. Everyone except Agnes and Mira. They're searching the trees. Then I hear Kenosha's voice —not from her mouth, from the wind:

"But we all make mistakes. Winona's house was mine. In order to stop Alondra, I cursed it. I thought that a little evil for the sake of a little good was the right thing to do. It never is. My magic and Winona's empathic power was enough to damn the ground. That's what you saw me fighting. See, I wasn't just fighting Alondra, Cadence, I was fighting the evil in that house."

"*What is evil?*" croaks a voice. "*Why don't you tell the class, Cadence.*"

"She's here," says Agnes. "Quick, stand up and hold hands,

witches. She's attacking your hallowed ground. Recite these words, sisters: *relinquo, relinquo, vade retro daemonium.*"

"*What is evil?*" asks Melanie again through the wind.

"Recite these words," commands Agnes. "*Relinquo, relinquo, vade retro damonium.*"

"*Relinquo, relinquo, vade retro damonium.*"

I try to repeat the words with my sisters, but then it feels like something's splitting my head open. I fall to the ground, crying out in pain. Frida and Bryce rush to me and hold me. It's the worst headache I've ever felt.

"Don't break the circle!" cries Agnes. "Hold hands again! Speak the words again. Quick."

"I'm okay," I say to them, gently pushing them off. "Do as Andromeda says. Return to the group."

"Speak the words," Agnes says, desperate.

"*Relinquo, relinquo, vade retro daemonium.*"

"It's not working," Mira says. She is shaking her head, looking totally freaked out. "It's not." She looks all around her. "I feel her everywhere."

Agnes, that sweet old lady, jumps up from her chair, furious, jerking her head back and forth. "*Vade retro, daemonium!*" she cries at the trees. "*Vade retro!*"

"*Quel demon, headmaster?*" croaks a voice in the air. "*Qu'est-ce qui ne va pas ma chère Cadence? Vous toutes m'avez gâché la vie, assises ici prêtes à chasser ces soit-disant démons. Regarde-toi dans la glace! Mes oreilles en ont assez de ce bavardage incessant. Maudits soient les catholiques fourbes, ces immondes menteurs!*"

Then my whole coven bursts out in laughter. Even Bryce and Frida are laughing like crazy. Everyone's laughing except Mira, the head witches, and me. Thankfully, the pain in my head has left me. Now I'm just horrified. This is my coven. This is my hallowed ground. My circle once gave me enough strength to levitate in the air, but now I don't feel magic. I feel weak and afraid. I don't think I've ever felt so afraid in my life.

"Try me," croaks a voice in the wind. "Say something again, witches," mocks the voice. "It entertains us. How about something far older than Latin: *Meho Rua? Meho Rua?*"

I look around and all I see are the shadows of trees. These shadows usually comfort me, but now they feel dark and cold.

"What is evil? It's me! It's me!"

"Cadence," Agnes cries, whirling back to me in a panic. "Recite the first words of your meeting again. Your coven's greeting. Hurry! Say the words—"

There's a shearing sound, as if a wall is being torn apart. How? We're outside. Then the ground in my backyard quakes. White clouds race across the sky at unnatural speed, darkening the half moon. Then I hear cracks of thunder. It starts pouring. I believe I'm the one willing this rain, but I don't have any control over my powers. Why would I want a storm now? Wind picks up, and we all jump up from our chairs, some of which are being knocked over. Then it pours so hard that it douses the flames in our bonfire. That only makes it darker.

"So you're dying, Alondra!" my voice shouts in the wind. It's not from my lips, it's emanating from the trees. It's my voice from the past. *"Why didn't you tell me in the library? Why not tell me like a normal person!"*

"This is dark magic, Cadence!" cries Agnes. The wind whips her long white hair, nearly throwing her to the ground. "Cast right-sided magic. Speak love in your circle. Cast love. Hold hands with your friends and say the words *blessed be the day that the circle...*" She gesticulates for me to speak. I can't believe the old woman can stand amid this gale. All of us are being blown over. I'm on my knees. "Say it! Speak the words. Quick, Windstorm. Speak of your love for your circle."

"Get out of my head, Allie!" screams Kenosha, falling to the ground.

"Blessed be the day that the circle is brought together once more," I say. All my witches, some on their knees, others fighting to stand, are trying to recite the words with me, but I spoke unnaturally fast without emotion. I try again. "Blessed be the coven under our gods Gaia, Selene, and Astraeus. Blessed be. May you all never thirst."

"*I'm going to make you thirst, you fucking piece of shit! Little Katie's gonna be taken to Sheol in her own teacher's yard. She'll drag all you sinners down to burning hellfire where you belong!*"

"*Ignore Mud!*" Agnes says, shaking her head at me. "Say the words, *blessed be the day.*" She adds amid the incantation, "Say it and ignore her. Say it again, Cadence. Try. Say *Blessed be the day—*"

"*Inform your council that I thirst for sinners' blood!*" I cry, pointing an extended arm at Agnes. The words aren't from the air this time, they're from my lips. "*How dare you encroach on my circle, you feeble old woman! I told you never to enter my grounds again! You are forbidden here. You once said that yourself. Why are you even here!*"

Agnes is launched into the air. She lands ten feet from us in the grass. Then she starts convulsing on the ground. Kenosha, who seems to have recovered from her head pain, rushes through the wind to be by her side.

"Tell them, Allie," I say in my own voice with a laugh. "Tell them what you think of them. Go ahead. Tell them how much you hate the witches in the council. You wanted to kill them. Remember? Hypocrites. They attacked your lover. They sent a demon inside him. What do you want to do to them after they did that? What do you want to do to the so-called *council*? How about their headmaster?"

"My god, Cadence, stop it!" Kenosha cries. "You're hurting Agnes! Your magic is hurting her!"

"She's hurt," say all my witches in mockery. "She's hurt. My god, what do we do?"

Kenosha clutches Agnes in her arms. "Stop it! Please!"

Agnes is only shaking more. Through the rain, I see her eyes rolling back.

"How dare you enter my circle," I say in Alondra's voice again. "I told you once that you are never welcome here!"

"The possession's inside you, Cadence!" cries Kenosha, looking up desperately. "Stop her. Alondra is possessing you, Windstorm, with Melanie's magic. You can stop this! Stop it before you hurt her!"

"This isn't a possession! It's me. It's me!"

Kenosha clutches her head again, rolling in the wet, wild grass beside Agnes. Meanwhile my coven is standing over the two witches, just watching them suffer.

"We should have killed you when we had the chance, Willow," I shout at them. "I don't want you here, and I certainly have no interest in entertaining that old crow!"

She's stupid! Yes? Tell her. Tell her, Allie. Take away the intruder's last breath. Finish her off!

"Alondra," shouts Mira, on her knees, grabbing me by my shoulders. Her hair is flying in the wind. "Alondra. Teacher. Or Cadence! Help get rid of the offender in our circle! Please, Falconsong. Windstorm! Melanie is here. Tell her to go away! This isn't her hallowed ground. It's not Kenosha's or Agnes's grounds, but it's certainly not Melanie's! Cast a spell and tell the Samhain Witch to leave. *You* have to cast her out, Cadence! No one else can. Hawthorne is your grounds. *Vade retro! Vade retro! Tell her!"*

"*Vade retro, daemonium,*" I say with a slow nod, almost in a whisper, to Mira. "*Vade retro.*" But I feel so weak. I fall to my side, barely able to open my eyes... I can't keep them open.

"Tell her!" cries Mira desperately.

"Vade retro. Vade retro. Vade retro... Vade... everything and... Vade everyone."

～

"Is she breathing? I don't think she's breathing."

"No."

Allie, save them. Please.

You don't know the pain they once gave me, Cadence.

You never hurt them before. This isn't you, it's Abaddon.

I am Abaddon.

"Cadence collapsed too!" cries Mira. "My god, is she okay, Bryce! Bryce, look, Katie's on the ground unconscious. She won't move either!"

"But the Abaddon witch has left her from her incantation," Frida's voice says. Frida is frantic. But I can't see her. I can't see anything. All I can do is hear them.

"Cadence?" asks Bryce. "Cadence?" I feel him touch my face. "Cadence. God, please, open your eyes, babe! Please open your eyes."

"Kenosha's not moving!"

"It's not Melanie, Bryce," I mutter. I start weeping. But I still can't open my eyes. "It's not her. It's me. I tell you, Alondra's trying. She didn't mean to do this. God, I didn't mean to do it."

"I don't think she's breathing."

"Kenosha?"

"Both of them."

"Call 911."

"Agnes! Agnes!"

"*I don't hear her breathing at all!*" cries Maddie.

"I only hear laughter," I whisper.

12

THE WITCH INSIDE ME

I'm sitting on a couch in Aunt Jane's living room sipping tea. I don't know what's in the tea, I don't really care, but it tastes good. Jane's place is a total pigsty. She usually throws everything under rugs before guests arrive, but she couldn't do it this time. My coven's visit was unplanned. (I mean, you don't think we wanted to be anywhere near my house, do you?)

Everything's shit, but Jane knows her tea. Just like she knows wine.

Frida's sitting in a chair across from me. She holds a silver crucifix and brown beads in her hand, praying to God. I'm Catholic too, but I barely know these prayers. Frida's the most Christian of all of us, you know. But right now, my sweetest friend looks real sick. She tries to smile at me when I glance over—because she's Frida—but then she quickly resumes running her fingers over the beads and chanting to herself.

Madison's staring at her small backyard, leaning on the sliding glass door, holding a mug of the same incredible mystery brew. She doesn't look over, but in her profile, I see tears running down her cheek. Bryce is across from me, standing by a table and lamp, staring at his fingers, while Mira's leaning against a wall beside him. The rest of our gang went home, but it was weird, you know, because it was like the coven didn't want to go home. They kept looking to me. Because I'm their leader. But I didn't know what the fuck to do. I can barely talk to you right now, if you want to know the truth.

I cry. I do that on occasion. No one comforts me because they've been weeping on and off too.

"Are you feeling better?" Maddie asks me.

Before I say something mean, we hear the front door open. I'm expecting Maddie's mom to walk into the living room. It isn't. It's Dad, of all people. That's weird. But I don't care. I run into his arms.

"You're back, Dad?"

"Yes, Cadence," he says quietly in my ear, squeezing me tightly. "Because of everything going on."

Does he know what happened? That means he understands that my magic is real. I suppose he saw my eyes turn green a few weeks ago.

Then, far weirder, a man about Dad's age walks into the room. He's wearing a Yankee baseball cap and blue jeans, totally different from my dad's dark button-down and slacks. When he takes off the cap, I see his graying feathery auburn hair. It's the hair Allie's so crazy over. But, unlike in New Jersey, he's clean-shaven. Following Liam is Aunt Jane.

"Hi Cadence," Liam says quietly with a nod. He turns to everybody in the living room and waves uncomfortably.

To my surprise, Mira comes up and introduces herself to him. I always felt like Mira and Alondra were so close that she would have met him already.

"Why are you here?" I ask Liam, interrupting them. That sounds rude, but I really don't get it.

"Kenosha and I were good friends."

"*Were!*" I snap. "*Oh, my god, did Kenosha die?*"

"No, no, she's alive. But she's sick."

"She had a heart attack, Cadence," Aunt Jane says. "But she's doing all right."

"From my magic. I'm afraid I'm putting us all in danger until I figure out how to control it. Is that why you finally came here, Lee?"

"No," Liam says, shaking his head. "I told you, I swore to never cast magic again."

I plop down near Frida again. She's shaking with her head in her hands. I think she's crying again. I put my arm around her.

"Then why are you back?" I ask Liam again. Am I being a bitch? Maybe. But really, *why is he here?*

"I can help with magic, Cadence," Jane says with a shrug. "I only swore to never cast magic with Allie."

"Yeah, Mom's a witch, guys," Maddie says with a shrug.

"Why didn't you tell us before?"

"Allie's magnetic," Jane answers. "You can only stay away from her for so long. It's her charm, but it's also her curse. I had to stay away. But after leaving her coven, I never gave up being a witch, Cadence. I'm a green witch now, working with my love for the earth. With Alondra, all her magic turned dark. But you have to understand, when you attended college, I didn't know what was going on with Maddie and you."

"You don't have to talk about it, Mom," says Maddie.

"I think I do. I knew Madison was dabbling in witchcraft, Cadence, but there's a lot of witches in these parts. Had I known you two were with Alondra, I would have put a stop to it. But I had already been too rough on Madison after I heard she was in Alondra's history class. Alondra never understood why I left her. She always took my departure personally. She didn't understand that I knew if I ever saw her again, I'd come right back to her. But..." She smiles wryly. "At the risk of bringing her back inside you, Cadence, tell her she was right. If a witch is threatening you and your friends here in Hawthorne, I'm here to help you."

"We know, Mom," Maddie says.

I hear a whimper from Frida.

"Oh, Frida, are you okay?" I ask.

She shakes her head, crying some more. Then she says very quietly, "That woman was such a nice lady, Katie. She was so nice to me. Why did that have to happen to her?"

"Alondra taught me some black magic, guys," Mira chimes in. "I can help fight this witch. I'm all in with this witch war. But Mr. Johansen, if you were Alondra's husband, and she initiated you, you should fight too."

"There can't be any more fighting!" Frida yells, shaking her head like crazy. I've never even heard her shout. "No more meetings! No more sabbaths! No more people getting hurt!"

Then Frida falls apart.

"Okay, Frida," I say, giving her a tight squeeze. "Okay. I'm sorry. Forget it."

"It's not your fault, Katie," she says.

But actually, it is my fault.

I get up and walk outside feeling absolutely awful. Then I close the sliding glass door behind me.

It's sunny with clear skies. A nice morning despite my somber mood. Of course, all of us are exhausted. None of us slept last night. Maddie's backyard is small, like Liam's, but unlike his cement yard Maddie's has a lovely garden. It also smells wonderful. All the trees and grass are perfectly groomed because, as Aunt Jane just said, she's a green witch. Why didn't I ever see that before? That must be why the inside of the house is always such a mess.

"Allie used to tell me she runs," I overhear Liam quip through a crack in the sliding door. Jeesh, that sounds mean.

"Because of all that's happened, Lee," Jane replies, defending me. "Rick, I'll explain all this later."

Why does she have to explain anything to my dad? Why the hell is my dad even here?

I sit on a wooden garden chair looking down at some lilies. The white petals have fallen to the ground, so I pick one up and run the soft leaves along my fingertips. But that's bad because I see the white flower petal pass my black nail polish. Then I become even angrier as I realize I'm still holding my book, *Broomstick*, tucked in my other arm.

The glass door opens and, of all people, Liam walks outside. He looks up at the clear morning sky, then he slides a chair beside me. He removes his cap and takes a deep breath.

This guy is such a mystery. One minute he's swearing by his life never to come here, the next minute he's at Aunt Jane's house. It's like he was just making fun of me a second ago, over walking out on everybody, only to come out and join me. I find him so confusing.

He picks up a white lily from the ground, just like I did. I suppose he was once a witch who loved nature too.

"You want me to leave you alone?" he asks.

"I've missed you so much, Lee," I say quietly in Alondra's voice.

"I won't talk to her," he says, shaking his head. "We've been through this. Look at me, *Cadence*."

I turn. Under the shade of his baseball cap, his eyes grow larger. I smile while he scowls.

"Change your eyes back," he says.

"But aren't they pretty?" I ask, blinking stupidly. "You always said you liked my eyes."

He looks down.

Not now, Alondra!

"You saw Kenosha?" Thankfully, it's my voice again.

"Yes. The doctors think she'll make it. They're sending her to Atlanta for a procedure for her heart. Actually, Cadence, she wouldn't stop talking about you. She's so worried. With her heart, she can't get worked up. It was all Jane and I could do to just calm her down and get her to stop talking about you."

"I don't like her."

"I didn't like her once either," he says with a chuckle. "She planted a demon inside me."

"She did! Kenosha said she cast a spell on Alondra, but she never told me she put a demon inside you. That bitch! What other horrible things did she do?"

"Good, I see your eyes are back to normal. Yeah, Allie and I hated her. Actually, Allie nearly killed her in your backyard."

"Kenosha said Alondra was evil."

"You know Alondra was evil."

"That's why you left her," I say with a nod.

"Alondra's charisma draws you in," he says. "She's magnetic, just like Jane says. At first, I helped her stay balanced. She was already deep in the dark arts. Later, when I learned those same dark spells, we had no one to help us. Things fell apart. As did the town. And by then, after I brought my friend, I lost everything. A lot if it was because of that book." He taps the book under my arm.

"Throw the damn thing in the fire!" I say, handing it to him.

"I don't want it either," he says with a laugh. "It can be used for backward magic. But it can also be good, Cadence.

"Let me tell you something. When Alondra and I were having our most difficult time together, I saw you through the book. The book gave me a vision that offered hope.

"You were sitting in a black robe before a bonfire in our backyard. At first, I thought you were my wife, but then I noticed your darker complexion. Yet you held an intent I had seen countless times before in my wife. I realized it wasn't dark outside. The sun was bright and it was a clear sky. As I gazed at you in the vision, I wondered if you were my daughter. You didn't look like Alondra, but you acted like her.

"You see, Cadence, it wasn't only the coven that tore Allie

and me apart, it was her condition. My wife couldn't get pregnant. I was convinced the book was giving me the hope we needed at the toughest time in our marriage, telling me that we would have a daughter. It gave us both a little hope during a very difficult time—for a little while anyway."

"That's the prophecy Agnes spoke of?"

"Prophecy? Yeah, Andromeda called it that. But I always thought of it as just hope. Later, even when all was completely lost, Alondra and I still clung to this hope. That's why I returned her book to her to give to you." He looks down and runs his fingers along the flower petals he is still holding. Then he drops them. "I know what happened to Agnes at your sabbath was horrible. Believe me or not, I've cast my share of bad spells, many far worse. I've done things you would consider horrific. It's your choice if you want to continue witchcraft. I made my decision."

"But why'd you come back?"

"Agnes always seemed to keep things together," he says with a shrug. Then he furrows his brow. "Even when Allie and I were lost, Agnes was a force that made me feel safe. With her gone and Kenosha sick, Jane called. Then I believed you. I realized something terrible was happening in Hawthorne and that you weren't safe. But I can't show you magic. I won't do that." He taps the book again. "You really don't need my magic. You need the magic that shines already inside you. Not rage. The magic Alondra taught you. Remember, she was the one who always said *Lux alba* in her circle. White light."

"I remember Alondra telling me something about that when she was dying."

"One last thing," he says with a nod, getting up. "I said Alondra was your mother back home, not because Alondra was there for you as a substitute after the passing of your real mom. I was talking about Allie. Allie was the one who needed you *as her daughter*. Every call, every email, I had with Alondra in her last days spoke of you. She loved you, Cadence. Not only were you here to fix Hawthorne, you were here for her. Because you really were her daughter. Not just her favorite student, her daughter. Alondra loved you."

And that hurts. It's as if her spirit inside has been trying to tell me that all along but couldn't. Alondra never really could tell me things. She was always too closed off. She would confuse me, make me feel bad, and then make me feel this compassion and love at all the wrong times. In fact, the only time she told me something like this was the moment before she died, but, as usual, it was too late.

Alondra, you were so difficult!

But I feel your presence now. Your love.

"The Samhain Witch isn't making Alondra possess you, Cadence. You are. You want my wife inside you. But that needs to stop. You have to let her go."

But I don't want to let her go. In fact, I answer him by throwing my arms around him. He's made me finally feel happy! I feel like I can't control this joy. And I feel like you, Alondra, are here now, right? You're inside spurring me on to touch him. To feel him. To kiss him. I felt so horrible after last night. Now, finally, this man makes me feel good again.

I'm making out with him. I run my hand through his hair as I keep touching his soft lips. Then I squeeze his butt and press him so close. He's hot like Bryce, and I'm remembering being lifted in his arms while he was fucking me. I want him to do that now. I just want him to lift me up into his arms and fuck me. I want him as close as we can possibly be. Finally, to just be close to him again—

"What are you doing!"

"It's been too long," I mutter between kisses. I run my tongue along his. "I missed you. I love you."

"Allie," Liam says, shaking his head. "Allie? God. You can control this too, Cadence!"

"I miss you, Lee! Hold me. Feel me. It's me, Liam. It's me."

"*Prohibe!*" Liam cries.

My body is thrown from his arms, and I slide across the backyard, knocking down a small tree and a few potted plants.

All my friends run outside.

"I'm sorry," I say, putting my hand over my face in shame. "I'm so sorry."

"She can't control herself, Lee," Jane says. "It's a spell. It's not her fault."

"Jesus...it's..." Liam says. Through cracks in my fingers, I see him shaking his head. "Okay. I'm okay. I'm fine. I get it."

But Liam rushes back inside the house.

Bryce, of all people, helps me up onto my knees. He has this odd expression of shock and care mixed with anger.

"I'm sorry, Bryce. I couldn't control it."

"Your eyes are still green," Bryce says in disgust.

13

GRIGORI

I hate witchcraft, okay? You want to be me? Well, that makes you even more fucking weird than I am.

I didn't go off on a witch wandering after making out with Liam in front of my friends and my husband. Though completely humiliated once again, I didn't slip into a trance. Because I want nothing to do anymore with witchcraft. So everything's back to "normal." Right?

Wrong. I killed a sweet old woman. No matter what anyone wants to say, the spell came from my lips. And, like I told Agnes and Kenosha, I have complete control over you, Alondra. Right?

Well, enough negative shit. Time to think more positive thoughts.

One thing that makes me happy is clear skies and nice weather. It's close to Ostara, you know, which means it's getting warmer and nice enough to sit outdoors. So that's what I'm doing right now with my study group. I'm sitting with my students in the courtyard outside the student coffee house, at a bunch of tables with cute burgundy umbrellas, teaching. And I love it. I might not be all well in the head, but I can still teach.

I take a sip of my green tea latte.

Oh, yeah, and I love green tea lattes too.

"Grigori," I say. Then I nod to about twelve students sitting in a circle around me. "Grigori Rasputin, let's talk about him, guys. Anyone want to go over some of his antics? He was powerful after gaining favor with Czar Nicholas II."

A student with long blond and pink hair starts reviewing facts from Bryce's lecture. I drift off enjoying the view over the grassy knoll again, just like I did when I met with Maddie at the café. Then it was snowing. Now it's warm and the green, manicured lawn surrounded by our woods, unnatural or not, is so lovely.

I take another sip of tea.

Then a boy named Elijah, with small round glasses and a preppy button-down, starts talking about Czars.

Hmm... Of course, I hate some of my memories of this field. Down on the grass, legend tells of a full-fledged witch showdown last year. There was. It was me and a devil-worshipping horrible bitch-witch named Enora.

Good thoughts, Katie. Good thoughts. Cast away the negative.

What ever happened to Enora, anyway? She popped up at the Samhain Witch's house even after Kenosha had thrown her in jail. Then she burst into birds and escaped being killed by the Samhain Witch. So where did she go? And why am I thinking of her now?

Amica. Amica.

"Why do they call the old Russian leaders Czars?" I blurt out. I think I ask mostly to get my mind off that wicked witch.

"*Czar* is derived from the Latin word Caesar," says Lucas. "It's like *king*, Ms. Wallace."

"Yeah," I say with a nod, lowering my shades to look at him. "The Czar's family was a royal family. Remember the picture Dr. Wallace showed of his family? On July 17, 1918, Bolsheviks, likely under the orders of Vladimir Lenin, had the royal family stand by a wall in their palace and pose for pictures. The entire family was lined up. Then they were executed by a firing squad. It's a horrible photo when you know the consequences to the family afterward. But my question to you guys is, was the Czar, or king, killed off by his own actions or by his relations in court with Rasputin? Connect the two and talk about them because..." I smile and wink. " There just might be a connection brought up on the final exam."

"Know of Grigori. Grigori Rasputin was born a peasant. Then, in the late 1800s, he went on a pilgrimage, abandoning his family. He became a vegetarian and swore off alcohol. Some believe that it was on his wanderings that he learned of that underground Christian sect of the Khlysty. Whether he was a member we don't know, but we know he learned from their practices. And the Khlysty group is interesting because they dance in a trance, just like the Vodun of Benin. So...who knows, there could be a question about this sect, the Khlysty group, on the exam too."

You know, the function of these study groups is not only to review the professor's material, it's also a handy way to reward students who come to my study group with hints about what to study for their exam.

A woman in a pitch-black dress with black lace covering her neck and sleeves stands over Lucas across from my table. All that black reminds me of our robes. Then I lurch back when I recognize her lovely, wicked face and bright blue eyes. This is the witch who I hurled across the grassy hill last year. She also sliced my friend Mira's throat and tried to kill Bryce. It's Enora.

"Hi Katie," Enora says with a stupid grin. She looks down at the other students, wrinkling her nose. "I hope I'm not disturbing your class. Just figured I'd find you here. May I speak with you for a sec?"

I don't know what to say. I've lost the will to speak.

"Probably would be best to talk *away* from your students,"

she says with a nod, wrinkling her nose at the group again. "Not sure you want to talk about our private business."

"Let's take a break, guys."

I get up and rush down the walkway that meanders along the grassy hill. Of course, I have no intention of *talking*. I plan to get just far enough away from the kids to not be heard and then shout at her. When just out of earshot, I spin around.

"What do you want!"

She actually laughs.

"I heard what happened to the dean, Cadence."

"Yeah? Is that supposed to be funny? Were you part of the attack?"

"You saw me on Samhain. You know Mud wants me dead."

"You dare appear here on campus!"

"I've also heard you've been possessed by your teacher. I can speak with Alondra, if you'd prefer. She's inside you, right?" She starts studying my eyes. I'm really starting to hate when people do that. "You might not want to speak to me, but I made peace with Falconsong before she passed... if she passed. Perhaps she'll talk if you don't want to."

"Stay the fuck away from me and my business!"

My students, up the hill, are looking down at us.

"That beast is hunting us," Enora says with a smirk. "She killed Andromeda. She hurt Willow. I saw the whole thing through my black mirror."

"Do you see this lawn?" I ask, gesturing to the hillside. "Huh? Do you recall when I hurled you all the way across it?"

"Yeah. Ask yourself why I'd dare appear here before you again."

"Well, I have a class to teach," I say, turning my back on her and walking back up the hill. "I'm going back to it, and then I'm going to call the cops."

"I'll ignore your typical rudeness. I'm familiar with all the stress a witch can feel after she just killed somebody."

I whirl around again. Then I just stare at her. My stare alone sends her body tumbling over and rolling down the grassy hill. She stops about twenty feet down the hill. I spin around. God, did my students witness that? No, they're acting innocent enough, still studying.

"Katie," Enora says, getting up, laughing. "Katie." She just straightens her black dress. "Do you recall the last time I asked for a favor? Huh? I asked you to allow me to attend Alondra's funerary ceremony. Do you remember what happened when you said *no*?" My eyes bulge again. She puts her hand up, walking closer. "Agnes and Kenosha were my friends. We all worship under Selene, whether we dislike each other or not. We respect one another. I even respect you. But not that beast. Mud is hunting us. We have to work together, just like you worked with me to fight Reardon."

"You tricked me with Reardon and killed him, Enora!"

"He turned you into a snake, if I remember. I changed you back."

"You killed him and then you tried to kill Bryce!"

"Nobody's perfect," she says with a laugh. "Hey, listen, you really wanted Reardon dead too. And attacking Bryce was just a bonus. I might have gone a little too far, I suppose. Okay? Sorry. But..."

"And Mira?"

"Cadence, you and Mira hate each other. Look, fighting with one another is what the Samhain Witch wants. Ask yourself why I risked coming here? I know it's your hallowed ground. You can go throw me down the hill a few more times if you'd like, but I'm getting desperate. I can help you, Jane, and the High Priest. That beast is going after everyone with power from Alondra's past because Alondra's not here to protect us. She's even trying to bring back Alondra's Oungan."

Oungan... No one's even told me what an oungan is. How does Enora know that word?

"Ask yourself why Alondra is possessing you. Ask why she's asking for Liam, her High Priest, her oungan, to return to Hawthorne, when you know that Alondra couldn't get her former husband to return when she was on her death bed. Alondra summoned me before she died. She wanted to make amends with me. Why could she make amends with me, but not him? Her former husband? Interesting, isn't it? Must be something important, Katie. Why is Alondra channeling through you to get to Liam and Jane? Alondra spoke to me and made her amends, but she couldn't reach them. But, you see, you can."

"I don't know. I don't know why Alondra keeps appearing. Kenosha thought she was a demon."

"Kenosha is a fucking idiot. Alondra is still here. She had way too many sins to pass beyond the spirit world. That's why her best friend and her husband, Jane and Liam, abandoned her. That was our biggest fight when she dismissed me. I told her she was only jealous over my affair with Reardon. I reminded her she was guilty of far worse sins in her lifetime. But you're stupid like Kenosha, right? You refuse to accept that your teacher isn't a goody two shoes like you."

That's exactly what Kenosha and Agnes told me. Even Liam said that.

I don't know. I can't care right now. I've got a class to attend to.

I look back up the grassy hill. Fortunately, my students are ignoring us, still studying.

I turn back to Enora's sapphire eyes, that beautiful face with eyes belonging to the most vile witch I've ever known. She tried to bleed me, kill Mira, and sacrifice my husband.

"*Stay away from Hawthorne!*"

"Sure, Katie," Enora says with a nod. "After you help me. Do you know how powerful Agnes was? She was more powerful than Alondra. Think about that when I leave. She was arguably the most powerful witch there ever was, maybe more than Escoba. Ask yourself how the Samhain Witch took her life. If Kenosha recovers, she'll probably scratch her head. That animal used your power because Agnes would never have thought to magically shield herself from you. It was not only an impressive feat of witchcraft, it was brilliant. It was probably the only way to kill that infernal old woman. And now the creature has trapped you. You can't hold a sabbath with other witches without worrying she'll use you again to kill someone else. Brilliant again."

I never thought about that. Even if Frida and some of the other witches are willing to come together again, I can't risk holding another ceremony knowing that at any minute Melanie could take over my mind and hurt one of us again.

"And how did this happen on your hallowed ground? If Kenosha recovers, ask her. Or ask one of the feeble old hags from their so-called witch council who will, undoubtedly, converge here when they hear of the death of their beloved leader. But you don't have to ask them. Ask me. Alondra's spirit is in you to fight Melanie. Alondra's ghost is trying to help. But the Samhain Witch is twisting everything around. You know, your teacher, deep down, has been wanting to kill Agnes and Kenosha for years. This is how the Samhain Witch used her to murder them. She used you and she even used Alondra's ghost. After all, it's Falconsong's hallowed ground. Maybe knowing that Agnes's death was due to Alondra's ghost makes you feel a little better, Katie?"

"I don't believe Alondra would have wanted them dead."

"Well, it was either Alondra or you. Believe whichever makes you feel comfy."

"I hate you," I snap. "Not only are you a criminal, you're evil."

"Glory be Satan." She winks, raising her left palm. Her palm has a black backward pentagram tattoo. "I study the

Lesser Keys of Solomon and practice rites of the backward pentacle, bitch. But now, I need help from goody-two-shoes Katie. Our teacher infernally chose you, not me, to lead the coven in this town. Something you proved last year by hurling me across this yard."

"How do you know all this? How'd you know about Alondra being inside me?"

"Scrying," Enora says with a condescending sigh. "And experience. You know, Cadence, I was supposed to be you before that sick-fuck Reardon ruined my relationship with our teacher. You might detest me but, believe it or not, Alondra was pretty stricken by me. Alondra had every intention of passing the circle to me. She trained me. And after she dismissed me, she didn't have time to train you. She should have kept me under her wing. You don't even like magic."

That's the first thing she said that I agree with.

"But now, it might do you some good to work with someone who loves our craft. Someone who doesn't only love it, like Raven, but one who holds as much talent as you."

I can't believe this. Enora cut me with a knife and planned to sacrifice my husband. Now she wants to work with me? I look back again at my students. They're still staring at books.

"Enora," I say, shaking my head, "I can't forgive—"

"I'm not asking for your forgiveness, you stupid cunt! I don't give a shit about you. I want to keep that beast from hurting me and my circle." She slaps her chest. "This is about me, Katie. I don't care about you, Bryce, or Hawthorne. It's about me. I tried to burn you all down, if you remember. I'd love to burn—"

That's it. She did try to burn us, didn't she? So why am I even talking to her. I turn my back on her and head back up the hill.

"I offer my services," she hollers. "You need black magic. I'm an Abaddon witch who can help you. Because of my connections, I might be the only one who can."

I stick up my middle finger.

"Hate you too, Katie," Enora hollers with a chuckle. "Tootles. I'll be keeping my eye on you through my black mirror. Do you even know what a black mirror is? Probably not. Just call me, then."

When I walk back up the grassy hill to my students, they're all getting up, stuffing backpacks, or placing their books under their arms.

"It's the end of class, Ms. Wallace," says a short-haired girl with glasses named Tracy.

"Oh, sorry, guys. Read up on Rasputin and remember those dates."

"Thanks, Ms. Wallace."

My phone buzzes in my purse. I don't recognize the number. The text reads: *BTW, here is my number. Got yours by divination. Try a mirror sometime. Or call.*

I really hate her.

14

VISITORS

A THICK WHITE FOG HAS ROLLED IN, AND MY FRONT PORCH IS shining yellow light on our decorative red wooden carriage. It's dark and a little creepy. Maybe the weather is influenced by my magic? I don't know. I'm so upset after seeing that bitch Enora —not that I wasn't already in a bad mood. I spent the rest of the afternoon studying. I have to remember that I'm in school. Right now it's a little after eleven.

As I walk through the front door, my fat gray cat, Whiskers, grazes along my leg. I hoist him up and hold him in my arms for a second, running my fingers through his soft fur, squeezing him tightly and kissing his head. There's a flickering candle to my left. I pass the dining room and find my hubby sitting at the head of the table, just like in that horrible vision I had. He's running his fingers through his hair and rummaging through a stack of papers by a candle. (We have lots of candles at our house. We're witches, okay?) Beside the papers is a laptop and a cup of coffee.

To his right our gorgeous floor-to-ceiling window looks out at the forests surrounding our house. Because the fog's thick, I can't see anything through the window tonight.

I stand over him, holding our cat.

"Honey, I'm home," I quip stupidly. Then I lean down and kiss his cheek.

"Hi, Cadence," he says sleepily. "You feeling okay? I really didn't want you leaving the house."

"I have to live, Bryce. I can't do nothing. That's how people go crazy."

I sit down beside him, still petting Whiskers's soft fur. He purrs on my lap. "That's what happened in 'The Yellow Wallpaper.' Ever read that short story? It's a great one."

"Huh?" he asks, looking at his screen again.

"'The Yellow Wallpaper.' I saw Enora, by the way.'"

"What?!"

Guess that got his attention.

"She came by during my study group to ask for help."

"She belongs in prison, Cadence! She tried to kill all of us. I told you that you shouldn't have left home today."

"Look at you," I say, pointing to his papers and old books strewn along the desk. I touch his hand. "You look so tired."

I rub his fingers, but he quickly pulls away.

"What's wrong?"

Oh, yeah...he saw me make out with Liam.

"Bryce, about what happened at Maddie's house. I..."

"Cadence, forget it." He heaves a sigh and runs his hand through his hair again. "What else can go wrong? Kenosha's in the hospital. Agnes died. Alondra is inside of you. With all that's happening, the last thing we need is Enora popping up."

Whiskers falls from my arms and scurries away.

"Have you heard from Kenosha? Is she still in the hospital?"

"I called. She was well enough to talk, which was something. She's doing okay, but it's going to take time for her to recover."

"Then why work so hard? God, Bryce, I don't want anything

to happen to her, but I also don't want you to slave like this anymore."

"What happened with Enora? What do you mean she wants our help?"

"She wants to fight the Samhain Witch with witchcraft. I told her to go fuck off."

"She better keep away this time," he says with a nod. "She has no business showing up on campus. She never would have pulled a stunt like that if Kenosha weren't sick."

He slowly drags his fingers over his computer touchpad, staring at the screen. I look over and catch a black and white picture of a man hanging from a gallows pole. Grisly.

"You have no classes tomorrow," he says. "Just stay home, babe. Please."

But before I can object, we hear a knock on the front door.

"At this time?" asks Bryce, furrowing his brow.

"I'll get it."

"No. I'll go. God knows what witch is out there this time."

As we walk to the foyer, I see Mira shuffling slowly in her dark robe down the hall near the guest room.

"Hi, Cadence," Mira says sleepily with a yawn. "Feeling better?"

She stayed the night because she's still in town. But she's also really worried about me. Enora said Mira and I are enemies. Bullshit. It's true we love fighting with one another, but we also love each other. Everything out of that evil witch's mouth is a lie.

There's more knocking before I can answer Mira.

"Who is it?" I ask.

"Afreyea," says a woman with a thick accent. "I am Aurora."

"Are you the Hawthorne Witch?" asks another woman's voice behind the door. She doesn't have an accent. "I am Olwyn. And our close friend here, Gala, accompanies us from Romania. Her blessed name under the moon is Isis. We've traveled very far to see the High Priestess of the Crescent Coven. Now the council comes to see the Hawthorne Witch."

"Forget it, Cadence," Bryce says in a hushed voice. "You just said Enora saw you today. It could be a trick."

"Their names are familiar, Bryce," Mira says. "Alondra used to mention a great and powerful witch named Afreyea. She visited a few times with Willow on their ghost haunts. These are very powerful witches."

Mira's excited. Bryce and I aren't.

I stand on tippy toes and look through our peephole. Under our yellow porch light is a motley crew of three women wearing odd clothes, not freaky cloaks like I figured they'd be wearing, but not normal clothes either. The clothing looks foreign, except maybe the central woman, who has on a brown sweater and slacks. To her left is a pale lady with a pink cloth tied over her long dark hair and a long white dress. On her right, a dark-skinned woman is wearing a bright blue headdress and a saffron dress. I start opening the latch, but Bryce puts a hand over mine.

"No, Katie," Bryce says in a hushed voice. Then he raises his voice. "Why don't you come back tomorrow?"

"There may not be a tomorrow," says Olwyn.

I open the door.

"Windstorm?" says Olwyn with a smile.

I nod.

All three women are old like Agnes. Well, not as old as Agnes, but older than Kenosha.

"Beautiful home," says the dark-skinned woman, looking around. She nods at me. "A do gangi a." She taps her chest. "Afreyea." She stares up at our elegant crystal chandelier and gasps. "Lights are beautiful."

"We've traveled far," says Olwyn. "Afreyea traveled from Benin in Africa. After the evil tidings with Andromeda, Afreyea is our headmaster. We came to make peace with Andromeda after her passing, but with all the evil tidings, we decided to visit you."

"Come in," I repeat with a nod. "This is my friend—"

"Raven," says Olwyn, looking at Mira.

"Have we met?" Mira asks, furrowing her brow.

"We've heard of you. You are the witch who loves Hecate above all else."

Mira smiles wide, definitely loving that.

We all make our way to my living room. There I plop down on a brown leather lounge chair. Afreyea and the lady from Romania sit on one of our maple-colored couches across from me, and Olwyn takes another leather lounge chair to my right. Behind me is the sliding glass door leading outside. When they're not all staring at me, which seems to be what these powerful witches always like to do, they're glancing over my shoulder at the backyard.

"Can I offer you tea?" I ask.

"Stay here, Cadence," Bryce says. "I'll get some tea." He seems angry. He's so tense lately. He hasn't been acting like himself.

"What a good 'usband," says Afreyea with a big smile.

"We saw Kenosha in Atlanta," says Olwyn as Bryce goes to the kitchen. "She was very weak. She is—"

"I feel so terrible for what happened," I interrupt. "God, how is she? I'm so worried about her, you don't even know."

"She's more worried about you," replies Gala with a chuckle.

"We should have come earlier, at the passing of your teacher," says Olwyn. "Of course, Alondra beckoned us when she was ill, but we live so far away. We were so sorry to hear what happened to her. Alondra was known throughout the whole world, you know, even by witches in other nations. We haven't been here in a very long time."

"You want something to eat?" I offer.

"No," Afreyea says with another smile. "We had fast food. It was very good. I had hamburger and fries. I remembered how good it was last time. It was very good."

"It wasn't that good, sister," says Olwyn with a laugh.

"It was very good," Afreyea repeats with a big grin.

"Afreyea lives near Cotonou in West Africa, Cadence," says Gala with a chuckle.

"It was good," Afreyea says with a shrug.

"I'm so sorry about what happened," I say. "I feel responsible."

"Your magic was used, Windstorm," Olwyn says, shaking her head. "It was not your conjuring. The council accepts this."

"Well, you can't hold a Summerland ceremony for Agnes here," I say with a sigh. "I don't think we can safely have a ceremony here ever again."

"We can hold our own ceremony," Olwyn answers. "But that is the reason why we've come. No witch should ever be barred from ceremony."

"You are being attacked," Gala says with a nod.

"Two fronts," Afreyea adds, raising two fingers with a nod.

"Yes," Olwyn says. "On one side, you fight the Samhain Witch, on the other you battle your teacher-spirit, Alondra."

"I'm not fighting Alondra. Kenosha thought I was possessed by Alondra and fighting her too. I allow her inside me."

"For Hawthorne?" Afreyea asks, "or cross?"

I shake my head, but I don't know what that means.

"Kenosha believed you were possessed by a demon, but Agnes told me before she died that she was not sure," Olwyn says. "Yes, it's possible you hold Alondra by choice. But that means that this struggle ends in you."

"Alondra and Cadence were very close," says Mira with a nod. She's just standing by the fireplace now.

"Not this close," Gala quips.

"What do I need to do to stop the Samhain Witch?" I ask. "I

didn't want to hurt Kenosha and I didn't want Agnes to die. I'm so angry. Now I just want to hurt Melanie."

Bryce walks in with a silver tray of teacups. He hands tea to all of us. I turn to my left and look out the window. I catch Mira's expression. She looks intense. She wants Melanie to pay too.

"It's very late," Bryce says to our guests. "Can't we speak later? Perhaps in the morning, ladies?"

"No time, High Priest," Afreyea says.

"You are angry, Windstorm?" asks Olwyn. "The council is furious. Many of us are performing spells and incantations as we speak, in private, throughout the world. But the Samhain Witch is very powerful. She has devoted her life, not only to the arts, but to revenge. Simple curses will not be enough. How do you curse mud?"

"Mud," Afreyea says with a nod.

"Mud," Gala says, nodding too.

And that reminds me of Enora. I heard her refer to the witch as "Mud" too.

"I should tell you guys," I say, "my problem is not only the Samhain Witch. I was visited earlier today by a witch who attacked our coven last year. Enora. She wants to fight that witch too."

Mira stares at me. Mira doesn't want Enora's help. She has a thin scar along her neck where the witch cut her throat.

"The council is aware of her presence," Olwyn says with a nod.

"Enora is a murderer," I say. "I would never help her."

"She practices left-sided magic," says Olwyn with a nod. "She cannot help you. But she did not approach you to help you, she needs *you* to help her."

"How?"

"You can help all of us," Gala says. "You are prophesied to do great things. But for now, we must contain the Samhain

Witch's power. Join us in Alabama tomorrow. You wish to fight her? So do we. Come with us to her home. We will cleanse her grounds. We will wash out *Mud*."

I turn from them and stare at my backyard—anywhere away from my guests. Honestly, I don't want to go anywhere near that place again.

"We don't want to be there either," Afreyea says with a chuckle.

"Did you read my mind?" I ask, quickly turning back.

"No, I see your face," Afreyea says with a big grin.

"We must go," Olwyn says. "What happened to your coven must never happen to any coven again. The council thinks Alondra's possession of you is related to her conjuring before she died, but we are unsure. Maybe Alondra conjured her presence before she went to the Summerland? But even if Alondra herself resides in you, it might not be enough. Not enough to cleanse—"

"Mud," Afreyea says with a nod.

"Mud," Olwyn echoes with a nod.

"You're not planning to wash away anything," says Mira, opening her eyes wide. "You're planning to destroy her hallowed ground."

"This one understands our arts well," says Gala.

"But you must understand more," Olwyn says, lifting a finger. She sips some tea and stares over my shoulder. "There exist two battles here in Hawthorne. Two fronts. One is Samhain, the other Hawthorne. One is young, the other very old. Both empower the monster. Alondra's spirit might believe she is helping you, but her past use of left-sided arts is defeating you. It has caused a major struggle inside you. You must battle both if we are to succeed. You have to fight Alondra too."

Olwyn turns to the other witches. They all nod. Afreyea lifts two fingers again.

"Like Mira said, I loved Alondra. I would never fight her."

"Perhaps you should reconsider," Olwyn says. Then she points to the window. "Let me tell you a story."

She points for me to look over my shoulder. I'm creeped out. With these witches, I'm worried they're going to conjure up some vampire or ghoul behind my back.

"Did you know that your ancestor Escoba Hawthorne held hoodoo ceremonies right outside this house? Many believe this second house was built for outside ceremonial use of the backyard, not for the house."

"Yes, I saw Escoba perform there once in a vision."

"Two hundred years ago," Olwyn says, "Escoba was one of the most powerful witches there ever was. Do you know the story of Escoba and Abigail?"

"I don't think anyone living here doesn't know that ghost story," Bryce says. He's back in the room, standing over me with folded arms.

"Escoba was a slave and had a child with her master, Josiah Billington, at the Billington House, yes? But you are related by blood, Cadence, to both Josiah and Escoba. Again, you are the fulcrum. Their son, Maverick, is your distant grandfather. Abigail was Josiah's wife. Escoba and Abigail attacked one another. Escoba cursed all of Abigail's descendants, killing all of her children. *But* Abigail had a sister. Abigail's sister is related to Alondra."

"Alondra told Cadence they were related," Mira says.

"We know Escoba was a founding witch of Kenosha's Crescent Coven in New Orleans," continues Olwyn. "Hence Kenosha is even connected to the curse. The story goes that Abigail went insane after Escoba cursed her and killed all of her children. But your teacher discovered this is not so. Abigail, like Escoba, was a witch. Abigail studied in the tradition of Celts, Escoba's tradition was Haitian. Both witches had wanderings, of course. They wandered under Selene, but any such wandering at the time would have appeared mad to the towns-people. Crazy. Correct?"

"Wanderings appear crazy to me now," I reply with a nod.

"Do you recall what Abigail did to Escoba?" asks Olwyn.

"Legend says she stabbed her to death in revenge," I say.

"Either by Abigail's hand or by magic, yes. Abigail killed her."

But then Olwyn falls silent. She sips her tea.

"So?" I coax.

"Cadence, how do you think this stabbing made Escoba's spirit feel? How do you think it makes *you*, deep down in your soul, feel, Cadence Hawthorne, descendant of Escoba Hawthorne? You don't understand your struggle. This struggle is not just between you and Samhain. You belong to an ancient struggle between Escoba and Abigail. You are part of an ancestral curse."

"You and teacher are family, yes?" asks Afreyea with a nod. "Put together in family, not by blood, but by a fight. It is ancestor curse." Then she raises two fingers again. "Two fronts."

"An ancestor curse," says Olwyn. "Formed by two powerful witches in Hawthorne. The curse lies in your soul, passed from generation to generation. Your love for Alondra cannot take away the murder of Escoba, just as your love cannot remove Escoba's murder of Abigail's children. The spirits rage against each other inside you, Windstorm. Alondra might think she's helping the town, but her dark magic and your ancestor curse are harming you. There is love, but there is also bitter hatred. And rage."

"Windstorm," says Afreyea with a nod.

"You believe your teacher is a positive force?" asks Olwyn. "That you loved each other? What if the council were to tell you she is a negative one? Do you see these two battles feeding off one another? The Samhain Witch grows from your struggle. She wishes it to manifest, just as it manifested during your sabbath. When you really think of it, yes, Alondra was your teacher and friend. But your souls rage as enemies."

"Two fronts," Afreyea says yet again, raising two fingers.

"But Alondra was good to me," I say. "We had our differences, but we loved each other."

"You never fought?" Afreyea asks with a smirk.

"Alondra and Cadence fought all the time," Mira says with a chuckle. "Cadence can be pretty irritating when you get to know her, but I don't think anyone loved each other more than Alondra and Cadence. Alondra told me this many times. Cadence was very special to her."

"Our triumvirate comes to cleanse both grounds." Olwyn closes her eyes with a nod. "With your help, by the magic of Kemet; salt, mercury, and sulfur; body, soul, and spirit; we will cast a capstone to snuff out this violet flame. But to do this, we need the one who stokes the fire." She opens her eyes and looks at me. "Windstorm. That is why you must accompany us. If you accompany us to Alabama and we succeed in destroying her hallowed ground, we can then cleanse Alondra from you after —if you allow it. Then all will finally be well with Hawthorne."

"So you came seeking *my* help?"

"Kenosha's too sick to help," Gala says. "But such a boastful question sounds left-sided."

"You all don't understand," snaps Bryce. "Cadence is having such a hard time, the last thing she needs is to go back there."

"But how else will this end, Bryce?" I ask. "What else can we do?"

"I'll go," says Mira. "You're right, Katie. We have to do something."

Bryce shakes his head vehemently.

"Will you hurt Melanie?" I ask.

The three witches look at me like I'm crazy.

"Melanie doesn't need to be destroyed, she needs our help," I say. "She's suffering. I saw it last Halloween. The Samhain

Witch is in pain. She is a monster, yes, but... I see that deep inside, she needs our help."

"This is your confusion, child," says Gala. "Your two-front battle. You cannot clean mud. All you can do is wash it away."

"Cadence is good," says Afreyea, smiling sweetly. "But Samhain fools you, child."

"No, I saw it," I say. "I tell you guys, Melanie is suffering."

"Pride," snaps Olwyn. "Do you doubt our words? Your teacher never trusted us either. You don't trust us now? You are speaking with the head witches of the world, Windstorm."

"I'm just saying what I saw."

"We tell you, that mud is not human," Olwyn says.

"Windstorm will balance," says Afreyea. "So says prophecy."

"Prophecy given by the greatest offender," replies Olwyn. "It might not be enough, headmaster."

"She is prophesied," says Gala, nodding.

"Prophesy or not, she might be used by this abomination," says Olwyn.

"I see goodness," says Afreyea, shaking her head. "Cadence is good."

"I'm right here, guys," I reply, waving a hand. "I don't want to go back to that house. Bryce is right. I'm not sure even you guys can stop the Samhain Witch. If you had seen the darkness inside her—"

"We feel her shadow every day," says Olwyn.

"I'll go if it's the only way," I say.

"You can't!" Bryce snaps. "No, she won't. She almost got killed there. I watched it. No. No, you can't go back there, Cadence. I can't permit this. After what happened in our sabbath, you want to go to her hallowed ground?"

"Bryce, this has to end," I insist, looking up at him.

He shakes his head again.

"Why can't my coven create a shield spell?" I suggest.

"You saw what happened when you held ceremony," Olwyn

says. "How can you cast anything with your sisters now? The Samhain Witch prevents you from holding sabbath. The only way is for us to come to her and destroy her hallowed ground. That will strand her. She will then only be able to wander."

"There is another way," says Afreyea, raising a finger. She smiles sadly at me. "She can give up the ghost."

"Yes," Olwyn says. "Very wise, Aurora. Another way would be to exorcise Alondra first, Windstorm. If you would allow that, the three of us could then hold ceremony with your coven and provide protection."

"You three need me."

There's silence. At first, I don't understand why. Their eyes are wide open. Afreyea and Gala are staring at walls, just like I did when I didn't want to look at them. It's like they're doing everything they can to avoid my gaze. Then I realize I said those words in Alondra's voice.

The only one in the room who seems to not be fazed is Bryce. He's furious. He storms out of the room.

"The council accepts," says Afreyea quietly, sounding shaken.

"Raven, if you wish, you may accompany us," says Olwyn.

I hear something fall in the kitchen. Then there's the sound of a dish clanging on a table. Bryce is full-on super-pissed.

Olwyn picks up her teacup with a shaky hand, and it clangs against its saucer. But what freaks me out is, I don't think Olwyn is upset about Bryce's temper tantrum in the kitchen. I think she's afraid of going tomorrow. Or...is she afraid of me?

15

THE WITCHING HOUR

I'm lying in bed, on my side, staring at a wall in the dark. I'm not sleeping. I see violet firelight emanating from the back-yard through our large bedroom window. Is that Alondra's spirit? Or Melanie's? I don't know. Of course, probably only my psycho-mind sees the purple flame.

Bryce quietly opens the door and sits on the side of our bed. He removes his robe and climbs in wearing only his underwear. It's warm enough for him to sleep like that. He thinks he needs to be quiet, but I told you, there's no sleeping for me tonight.

"Hi, Bryce. Sorry."

Behind me, he gently rubs my back.

"Why are you sorry, babe?"

"I heard you throwing things in the kitchen."

He laughs.

"You really want to go through with this tomorrow, Cadence?" he asks. "I think it's a horrible idea."

"Yes." I turn, and my hubby is leaning on his elbow under the covers. I can just make out his stubble and his eyes in the shadows. "It's the only way. But I will be with those powerful witches."

"Kenosha and Agnes were powerful witches. They couldn't manage her, and that was in our own backyard. I don't want you to go."

"Stay here then. Maddie agrees. She absolutely refuses to go with me. And I already heard an earful from her about going."

"If you're going, I'm going. I just don't want any of us going tomorrow."

"You know, you've been worried about me a lot lately," I say, pressing a finger to his nose. "You're acting like I'm pregnant or something."

"Cadence, do you have any idea what it was like when you went missing for three days after you left Maddie's house? It was almost as bad as when Reardon changed you—maybe not that bad—but whenever you're missing, it's horrible. That night you saw us in the living room wasn't just the night you came back. All of us, your dad, Maddie, Damie, Maddie's mom, all of us were holding vigil as if you had died." He shakes his head. "I don't want you leaving me like that anymore." He falls back on his pillow, looking at the ceiling. Then he takes a deep breath. "Cadence, I can't take that again."

"Okay."

"Kate, I never joined Alondra's coven for real magic. I joined because I shared Alondra's interest in ritual. Even before I knew the coven was the real thing, our teacher and High Priestess impressed me with her knowledge of witchcraft, but it was for knowledge, not practicing real magic. How much more of this can I take? How much more of this can you take? You joke about going crazy, both of us are going to go crazy if we have to keep fighting possessions, demons, and haunted houses. I love the circle. Our coven. Our friends. I like being a witch, but it's out of love for ritual, not fighting evil witches like Enora or demons and ghosts with magic. And now, my wife has my former teacher inside of her. It's just...it's just all too much to take."

"Okay."

What else can I say? I hardly disagree with him.

"You can't sleep?"

"I'm joining the *council*, whatever the hell that is, to drive to Alabama and revisit a haunted house from hell tomorrow. Nobody's sleeping, Bryce."

But I turn on my side and put my arms around him. Then I run my fingers through his hair. He has really cute hair. Like... Liam.

I hear Bryce quietly breathing. He's just lying in my arms, and I love that.

"Cadence," he says quietly, "you went to New York to find help from Alondra's first husband. You didn't find it. Then we had a ceremony that went nuts. Now we're trusting three strangers we've never met."

"I think I'm the one who's supposed to help Hawthorne," I say with a deep sigh, letting go of him. "I'm our High Priestess. Sorry for the disappointment."

"Oh, stop it. You're different from Alondra, but everyone in our coven loves and trusts you."

"Well, don't be asking for Alondra's help. I love Alondra, but I don't want her popping out now."

He actually laughs.

I turn my back to him, and he scratches my back. He knows I love it.

"What else can we do?" I ask with a shrug. "I feel like going with those three witches back to the house is the only thing to do."

"Then I'll go with you."

He presses his fingers deeper into my skin. I feel his hand slide over the nightgown and along my bare back, pressing even harder. That feels... so...good.

"Bryce, about Maddie's house. Liam and I—"

"Cadence, I know that was under a spell."

"You won't let me finish my sentence."

He stops yapping. But then he stops scratching my back.

"Bryce, sometimes I don't have control over her, but I know she's here to help us. With Liam, well, she loves him. So when she's in me and she sees him—"

"I get it."

"There you go again, interrupting me."

"I didn't say I liked it."

I laugh. He changes from scratching to rubbing my back. Massaging me. That feels even better.

"I'm sorry about kissing him, Bryce. I'm so sorry about you seeing that and hurting you. I don't love him. I love you."

He stops. I cock my head, and he gently kisses my lips. And that feels wonderful.

"If we kiss," he asks between kisses, "Alondra's not going to appear in our bed, right?"

"Ew, gross, Bryce! No!"

"But you said you don't have control."

"Alondra was irritating as hell when she was alive, but she was also proper. Remember?"

He nods.

"But..." I feel a large grin coming on. "How come you're asking?"

He shrugs. Then he gently turns me so that my back is turned to him again. His hand moves up to my neck. Then he's massaging my neck. He strokes my long hair and then kisses the back of my head.

"Do you see the purple firelight in our backyard tonight?" I ask.

"No," he says, kissing me some more.

Yep, I'm seeing things.

He reaches over and I turn my head. We lock our lips again and just kiss. That's nice: just running my tongue along his.

"You'll still love me when I go crazy?" I ask between kisses.

"Only if you still love me when I do. I will always love you, Cadence."

"Cadence Wallace. I'm your wife, hubby."

I lean up to kiss him again. He moves closer and enters my mouth again. And then we just keep smooching for a while. And it feels so nice. Then it's nicer when he runs his hand along the curve of my breast. And it feels even nicer when his hand roams inside my white lace nightgown and touches the skin along my curves and nipples.

"I love you, Cadence Wallace."

My hand glides down his back and slips inside his underwear. It rubs his hard cock. I feel so aroused. But I figure Bryce is even more aroused, judging from how hard he is. It's been a long time, too long, since we made love.

He gets up and climbs out of bed.

"Bryce," I say, snatching his wrist. "Wait. Where are you going?"

"Katie, I have to get a condom."

"No. Let's do it without this time. You want me. Take me. Take me as I am. I want you, Bryce. I will never want another man."

"But Cadence, are you sure?"

"You want me, baby or not? I want you. Do you? We've talked about it. It's okay."

He hesitates.

I tug him back onto the bed. Then we're at it again, smooching like crazy, this time facing each other. He gently squeezes my boob then makes his way farther down and slips his hand under my underwear, his fingers touching my pussy.

I moan.

"Oh, Cadence, I love you," he says between more kisses along my neck.

"I need you, tonight, Bryce. I need *you*. I've felt so terrible about what you saw at Maddie's. I never want to hurt you, Bryce. And lately I just feel like I'm losing it."

"You're not crazy, babe," he says, pulling off my panties. Then he squeezes my naked ass. "You're a witch. We're witches. Maybe we're not crazy, it's just that what we've become is crazy."

"But you know I don't want to be a witch. And I might not be crazy now, but..."

His underwear comes off.

With his strong arms, I feel myself turned onto my back.

He's touching my boobs and kissing my neck again. I'm cradling a pillow as he massages me again, sending kisses down my naked body. Then he gathers me up, squeezing me so tightly. I feel his cock glide along my leg. I pull off my white lace nightgown and throw it off my bed. We're both nude now. Then I turn over and pull him close. I feel his weight over me as he enters me.

"I love you, Cadence."

It's dark, but not too dark. The drapes are open, and behind my man I can still see the shadows of the forest in our backyard. The purple glow is there too. But it's peaceful. Not the violet light, the woods. The light, for a moment, makes me shudder. I recall the fear I felt when Melanie had taken over my coven. And I remember Jane warning me not to return to Alondra's house afterward. But what was I to do? Stay at Maddie's?

"Are you all right?" Bryce asks, breathless.

"Yes."

"Your head seems to be someplace else."

"There's a lot on my mind, honey. That's why I'm crazy. I'm as worried about tomorrow as you are."

"Don't think. Just be with me."

"That's easy, Bryce," I say with a chuckle.

And really, loving him is easy. Because he feels sooo good.

Well, not just that. I also love him to death.

The mattress creaks as he thrusts inside me harder. And I hear the wetness of our sex. That makes me groan more. I think I'm a bit too loud, because Bryce runs his fingers over my lips, covering them for a moment.

"Babe, Mira's still in our guest room," he says in a forced whisper.

Figures. The one night out of the whole month we're making love again, and one of our friends is staying over. My lips land on his again and that shuts me up.

I peek behind him, and that purple bonfire is out. It's just the dark trees. If I weren't a witch, perhaps that shadowy view would be frightening. But it isn't. If I weren't worried I'd lose Bryce's excitement, I'd suggest we rush downstairs, go outside, and fuck outdoors.

"Fuck me," I whisper. "Fuck your witch."

He presses deeper in response. All his weight is on me now. My hands run along his muscular back then massage it as he presses in. And I love it.

"Oh, Cadence."

"I'm going to cum, Bryce. Fuck...this is so nice. Just you over me, babe. It's what you wanted. Just you. Right?"

"Yes."

I pull him as close as I can. I love just hugging his hard body in a close embrace. His hips are pressing into me harder than ever. And that's driving me crazy.

I orgasm under him. He has to cover my mouth, I'm moaning so loudly... But...he's not done.

"I can pull away," he whispers in my ear.

"No. Love me. Do it, Bryce. Do it to me. Fuck me. If we make a baby, I'll love her so much. Just make love to me, husband."

He lifts me so that I'm on top of him. Then I lean over him with my tits over his face. I know he loves this position the most, for the view, and it won't be long before he orgasms. But he's getting me excited again too.

"What if it's a boy?" he says with a chuckle, running his hand through my hair, along my back, over my butt and the crack of my ass, while pressing up inside me. His fingers stroke along my curves.

"What... huh?"

"You said *her*. What if it's a boy?"

"Our first baby will be a girl."

That assuredness seems almost weird enough for me to stop. Alondra used to say she could read the future. She said all witches can follow the wheel of life, the seasons, and easily perform divination. But I just told him our firstborn will be a girl? That's pretty weird.

"Chandra is going to be beautiful, Bryce," I say breathlessly. "I just know it."

And that's creepier. Now I'm naming her.

He pulls my body so close to him, caressing my back and squeezing my ass, and I love it. I feel the pleasure inside and that makes me lose all thoughts of our visitor downstairs, the future, or my witchery. I don't care about anything anymore. Except Bryce.

I cry out in ecstasy. I just can't stop! He puts his fingers over my mouth again. I moan more with his hand over my mouth.

"Mira," he says in a forced whisper. "Shh. Remember, Cadence?"

"Fuck!" I don't care. "Yes." I'm pushing my hips down on him now, banging him so hard, grinding him over and over. I'm about to cum again. There's a loud clapping sound as I smack up and down on his cock. I think our bodies are just as loud as my moans now. I'm pressing into his body so hard. I want to be so close. "Fuck, Bryce. Yes, let's make a baby. Oh, fuck me! I'm cumming. Fuck...Yes! God, I love you so much, babe! Fuck me..."

Bryce and I orgasm together.

He falls to his side and we both lie down, panting.

"I'm so happy, Bryce," I say, breathless. "I'm so happy. God, Bryce, I love you. You mean everything to me!"

"I love you." He turns on his side facing me in the dark, leaning on his elbow again. "But...are you sure about our child? Are we really going to have a baby girl?"

"Yes. But she doesn't have to be named Chandra. I just loved that name when I met our new witch. I'd love to name her after her. I really like that name. Don't you? But we can name our daughter anything you want."

"But did we really," he pauses and runs his hand through my long hair, "just conceive her?"

"I don't know," I say, laughing. "I have no idea."

Bryce kisses my cheek. "I love that name."

"And I will always love you, Bryce."

I put my arms around him, squeezing him tightly. Then I just enjoy closing my eyes and lying in his arms. His warmth and his caress make me finally feel sleepy.

But I won't sleep tonight. Not with my morning plans.

I love you, Liam.

16

MUD

Bryce stops his old gray BMW before a rickety old wooden bridge. He has to drive slowly so we don't dive through the wooden planks and crash into the water below. The bridge is not much wider than his car. I hate seeing this bridge again. Not only is it always a legitimate danger to our lives, it was sort of the beginning of the Samhain Witch's freak show. But I don't hate Geneva Forest. All these trees are like home. Of course, as if the broken-down bridge weren't bad enough, at the end of the bridge is a wall of white fog. That looks hellishly ominous, too, like we're going to be swallowed by the white smoke after we cross over. Mira's black van is behind us. We wait for her and, like last Halloween, she's probably more worried than Bryce about falling through the wooden boards with her heavier van.

"She's here," says Afreyea, seated behind me, in her thick accent. That freaks me out. Gala is sitting beside her. Olwyn is with Mira. "You feel her?"

"No," Bryce grunts, but it actually sounds more like he's saying "yes."

Flakes of ice start hitting the windshield. Snow? In mid-

March? What the hell? Isn't all this fucking weird enough? There's not a cloud in the sky.

"It could totally be Hansel and Gretel, you know, Bryce," I say. "She could be luring us inside to eat us."

"I don't see candy," Bryce says, shaking his head. "That house, if you remember, was more like a fly-infested dung heap."

"Beelzebub," says Gala.

"Huh?" I ask.

"Beelzebub," Gala repeats in her Romanian accent. "Lord of the flies."

O-k-a-y. You know, these witches are supposed to protect us, right? We're supposed to have a full-on witch showdown and kick some witch ass. So why does Gala sound scared? Then, to make it worse, Afreyea is whispering. At first, I thought she was muttering something about Beelzebub. No, she's chanting an incantation in another language.

Ice now covers our windshield, and Bryce has to slow the car to a crawl and run his windshield wipers.

A rush of water splashes my passenger window and makes me jump. Did Bryce drive over a puddle? No, he has almost stopped. Is this the start of black magic shit?

I look back and see something I wish I hadn't. Afreyea's eyes are wide open. Apparently, the water splashing scared her.

"She's here," Afreyea says. "Brought your book, Cadence?"

Uh, I sure did.

"We end this now, Aurora," Gala says. "We finally end this, sister."

Bryce's car bumps like crazy driving over a broken road full of potholes and large rocks. Then, after we wind up a hill, we approach the address. But Bryce is forced to stop because he can't see the house or the road—rain and sleet are falling so hard. We can't see anything, but we should be there. Yes...wait... wind blows the ice, and I catch a glimpse of the familiar dung heap that is the Samhain Witch's house behind a white fog. Mud, indeed...or Beelzebub. Like last time, it's just a muddy shell of a home with tiles missing from a roof that's half caved in. All the windows are covered by leaves and filth. Saplings and brush are growing through the walls.

Someone throws open a car door in the back, making me jump again. Water rushes into the car.

"No, Afreyea!" Gala cries. "Not yet! Cast inside, sister."

Afreyea rushes by my window, her brown cloak turning darker after being drenched by ice and rain. Then she stands before the car, extending her arms and mouthing something as sleet splashes over her face and wind tries to throw her. I think I hear her say *"abaddon,"* but I'm not sure.

Bryce's whole car shakes in a rush of wind, and Afreyea is nearly toppled over. I can barely make out Mira's black van in my side mirror. Then I see Mira and Olwyn, in dark cloaks, struggling to get out of their car.

"Stay in the car until we signal for you, Windstorm," Gala says.

Hey, I'm not going anywhere.

Gala acts as nuts as Afreyea, fighting to open her passenger door and fighting the storm just to stand next to Afreyea in front of our car. She raises her extended arms, pushing her body against the gale.

Two black cloaks rush by Bryce's window: Mira and Olwyn, pushing to move forward. The wind is so strong that some of the tiles on the roof of the house are hurled toward the surrounding trees. The entire house shakes, and parts of a wall cave in. And the storm is only growing. I'm not sure whether this is Melanie's magic or the work of these four witches.

"Should we get out too?" I ask Bryce.

Bryce doesn't say anything. He's staring forward. Wait... he looks weird. He's not moving at all.

"Bryce! Are you okay? Should we get out—"

Lightning strikes, and all the witches in front of the car drop to the ground. They fight to stand.

Then they're at it again, extending both arms, closing their eyes and shouting chants. *"Abaddon! Abaddon!"*

More stones are thrown from the walls of the house.

I've been waiting all day for this witch showdown, and now I can't believe that Bryce and I are stuck in the middle of it without even leaving our car!

"Did you bring my book?" I ask Bryce.

Wait, why am I asking HIM that?

"Cadence, we have to talk."

The words are spoken behind me. It's not Bryce. Bryce is still frozen, staring ahead. No one else is in the car. It sounded like Kenosha.

"Cadence, we have to talk," Bryce mouths.

I hear children's laughter surrounding me. And a thousand whispers.

"Melanie? Melanie, is that you?"

All four witches somehow manage to stand up in the storm in front of our car. They raise their arms again. But then...their furling robes freeze. Everything freezes. Everything. The house stops crumbling, the wind stops blowing, and the witches and Bryce remain perfectly still. Bryce isn't even blinking. And ice crystals are no longer falling. They are frozen in time, hovering over the ground.

"Bryce? Bryce!"

He doesn't respond.

"Cadence, we have to talk."

I open the passenger door. There's a metallic-like sound as the door cracks through a wall of ice and rain frozen in time. I walk through the wall of ice. And it hurts. Every time I pass through frozen rain, the ice cracks against the skin of my hands, neck, and face. In fact, it creates a dry space where my body just emerged from the car.

Squinting, I can make out the cursed house of the Samhain Witch through a shimmering wall of ice. It's almost as if I'm looking at it through a mirror.

I pass Afreyea, Olwyn, Gala, and Mira. Their faces are completely frozen, intent on the house before them but motionless. Mira's mouth is open, casting some incantation. It's so quiet. Too quiet.

"Cadence, we have to talk."

All of a sudden, there's a loud thud, made tumultuous in the silence. All the ice and sleet crash to the ground as if a huge bucket was overturned. The sound of the fall is so loud that it's like an explosion echoed by surrounding trees. I turn, but the witches are still immobile, now drenched from the downpour of rain and ice. The storm is over. The broken-down haunted house lying before me is drenched, and my friends are still paralyzed in the midst of some weird witch incantation.

I head slowly toward the house, clutching my book tightly to my chest. More whispers echo from the woods. Then the sound of a baby crying.

"We need to talk."

"Melanie, yes, we do need to talk," I say. "I can help you."

"*J'ai attendu. Entrez par la porte, Hass-Horn.*" Then her voice changes to that of a little girl: "When my sister and I were playing one morning, Katie, we saw cards in a cupboard. The characters were funny." A little girl giggles. "It was with a few old books. The covers of the books were black and had pointy stars. There was a stick, a bunch of pretty colored stones, and a wooden cross. My sister and I played with the wand. At first, it was a lot of fun..."

"We need to end this, Melanie."

"It all ends with your sacrifice," Melanie croaks in her normal hideous voice.

I'm still not sure where she is. I'm looking everywhere, but it seems her voice is echoing around the woods surrounding the house.

"Look, Melanie—"

"Choose. Choose your sacrifice."

It's cold. I shiver. I realize that I ran out of the car so fast that I didn't even grab my cloak. I'm just in a dark green sweater and blue jeans. But I clutch my book. I'm not going anywhere without that.

"If you don't choose, I will," she croaks. "How about...*Bryce.*"

"*Don't you touch him!*"

"When you understand the arts, Katie," Melanie croaks with a laugh, "you learn that it becomes easy to stop the machine we call the body. Mendicants do it in meditation. Just a turn of a switch and they can slow down their heart or stop the air flowing in their lungs. They can hold their breath for minutes. More advanced wizards can cast this on others. Turn around, Cadence *Wallace.* I've devoted my entire life to the arts. Would you like me to show you?" I turn and Bryce is shaking in the front seat of our car. "Alondra once enjoyed this. Remember the fate of Andromeda?"

"*Okay! Let him go! Just stop it, Melanie!*"

"*Stop it, Melanie!*" cries a little girl's voice. "*Stop doing that! They're trying to help you!*"

"What do you want from me!" I shout.

"Careful. If you don't choose, his mind might not remain the same," Melanie says, chuckling.

"*Let him go!*"

I look back and Bryce stops shaking.

Then Melanie roars with laughter. The trees in the woods respond by moving their branches around as if they are laughing too.

"Perhaps Raven?" the monster ask. "But hasn't Raven suffered enough? All you witches suffer, don't you? Even the one you hate the most. Enora?"

"What about your mother!" I shout. "Kathy suffers because of you!"

"*Abaddon, Abaddon*, who suffers who?"

"Let us go! Stop attacking us. That's why we're here!"

"Who attacks whom? Choose the companion that dies. Then you may leave us."

"I won't choose that! Okay?" I cry, searching the trees surrounding us. "Look, we came so you will leave us alone."

"Hand someone or something of value to me, and I might let you go."

"I won't choose someone for you to murder!"

I search the trees. Finally, as I turn to my right, I see her crouched only a foot away from me. No, first I smell her. Her stench is an odd mix of rotting meat and excrement. Even all this storm water can't wash away that smell. Her closed eyes are dark, and her face and body are covered in filth. Mud and leaves cover her naked chest. Mud. Yes, mud, exactly as Afreyea described. As she approaches me, I see thin, dark serpents slowly moving along her neck.

"What is this?" she croaks. She opens her eyes, which look so white under the mud, staring at the book I'm clutching tightly in my arms. She taps it with her long, mangled nails. "Your Book of Shadows? Your grimoire? Did you dare bring your charm *again* to me?"

"Here," I say. I present *Broomstick* with outstretched hands. "Here's my sacrifice. No person. You can have my book. Take my book and just let me and my friends go."

"*You wish to hand me the book that destroyed us!*" she screams in my face. I recoil from her putrid breath. "*It was that book, that weapon, that Alondra used to kill my sister! You wish to hand that to me? This is your sacrifice? That is a pile of shit!*"

"It will give you power."

"I don't want power, you stupid li'l ewe. I want to watch all witches die."

"But we can burn it," suggests another voice. It sounds older and is coming from far off, in the direction of the house. Is sounds like her mother, Kathy. "We can burn it, Melanie."

"Yes, Momma," Melanie says with a nod. "Yes, we could burn it. That we could do. Hmm…"

She snatches the book from my hands.

"Don't hurt us. We'll leave. Just take the book and leave my friends alone."

"All I want…" She runs a finger along the spine. Then she opens the book and turns some pages with wide eyes. "All I ever wanted was for you to leave *me* alone. You offer this to me, little Katie *Hass-horn*? Why?"

"I never wanted it."

"No!" cries Olwyn. "Don't give her your book, Windstorm!"

Melanie snarls at the witches behind me. Somehow talking to me broke Melanie's spell on them, and I hear all the witches shouting "*Abaddon*" again. Melanie turns from them and returns to perusing my book with her dirty, misshapen fingernails.

"Don't give her the book!" cries Afreyea.

"It's your power, Cadence!" cries Mira. "You can't give that away! Remember when you handed it to Enora!"

"For me?" asks Melanie, putting a hand to her chest. Her smile disgusts me. "A gift for me, li'l Katie *Hassy-horn*? How sweet."

"Yes. Yes. You can have it. Just let us all go. Please."

"*The council accepts*," mocks the witch. "But in return…" She smiles, her gray lips wide, and raises a finger. "The headmaster dies."

There's a scream. I turn and Afreyea is on the ground convulsing.

"No!" I cry. "Leave her alone, Melanie!"

But Melanie's ignoring me. She's ignoring all of us, staring down at the book. She turns from me and slowly walks back toward her house. When she nears her broken front door, it opens by itself, then it slams shut behind her.

I can't chase her. My legs don't allow me to move forward.

All the witches have stopped their incantations and are surrounding Afreyea. Afreyea's sick, still shaking on the ground. I can't go toward the house, but I find I can run back.

"Afreyea, Afreyea!"

17

———

LILY DAISY FEET

FINE LONE CIGARETTE RIDES THROUGH BLACK WINDOWS CURDLED upon lone racks before the race tomorrow afraid fear darkness follows swallowing on the rise along a sunny shore where upon light turns dark, dark to light, Abaddon witch. The moon darkens white then brown, lighting a path by furnaces along dark caves and openings before frail, fine locks of nothing. Then, lark, comes light once more to brighten a path before dawn. But light exits only once, not twice, for those without raining hemp. I think there's masterful knowledge in knowing crab cakes and rivers streaming forward need only know sight from lightning.

"Shut up, Mother!"

Bright halls flowery without light. Come to me, ye witches and leave my sight. I see a train. Dead filled rushed and gone built upon a complete dark mess with tatters and pigeons line fray beat cars on roads remembering the day. Corpses or bodies or endless dead. Was it you, Winnie? Did you ruin my doll house?

"I have the book, Momma! I have it. Let's burn it! Let's go burn it to ash!"

"May I see it, dear?"

"No, stupid woman. You *may'nt see*. It's curs-ed I tell you. Curs-ed, like you!"

Did I spell our spell right?

Forged from light. Clouds form darkness. Brown surrounds a white moon. A beautiful defilement of honest tides like waves rippling across water of a beach now strewn cold.

Strange how every... word... I... think... of... appears... on... the... page.

"Did you hurt that sweet girl, Melanie?"

"Quiet!" I say. "*Not yet!*"

"Be a darling and make me a fire. It's cold, Melanie, and the water is dripping over my ass. We can sit by the flames and talk of the past, like we used to do with your sister and father, before needing the extra kindling. By the way, have you seen your sister?"

"Hear 'em? Do you hear them? They're crying! They're crying, Momma! Witches are crying over the death of another witch who tried to hurt me. Why sad?"

"'Fraid my hair's only dirtier this morning, Melanie. I'll have to trim the hedges."

There's a knock on the door.

"Momma, can you get the door? I'm busy reading *Broomstick*."

"I'm fixing my hair, dear."

But I know who's at the door.

"She brought the demon, Momma! Knew she would. Revenge is nigh! Feel it? Fulfillment is nigh! Finally gonna roast 'em witches and suck 'em dry to da bones!"

18

THE DEVIL

Two witches stand by the threshold of my front door wearing black cloaks. It reminds me of when I was a child and they came to help my sister, Winnie, and me. Do you remember, Momma? But these witches are middle-aged. They stink. I look down at my hands. My palms are covered with leaves and muck. Why are my nails long and my hands dirty?

The devil removes his cloak from his head, revealing reddish-gray hair. 'Course we know the vile devil. This is the wretch who came to our house with the Hawthorne Witch and Crescent Witch during our first haunting, but back then he wasn't a witch, Momma. *Yet.* But I don't know the lady. She has long gray-blond hair and stinks of vanilla and oranges.

"Give me the book," the red and gray haired demon says. "Hand me what's mine, Melanie."

It's him. It's him.

"Afreyea is sick," he says. "I need *Broomstick* to revive her. Give me that book and we'll leave. She needs my help."

Behind them is that stupid little ewe, Cadence Hassy-horn, the li'l witch that gave me her book, crouching over their lead witch crying and crying and crying. I laugh. It's so funny!

"Give me what is mine," the wizard repeats. "Give it to me now!"

"The Hawthorne Witch gave this book to me as her sacrifice, devil," I say. "The talisman is now my sacrifice for you and your friends' invasion. Otherwise, I kill all of you. I intend to burn this book in the fire. You may come in and watch its destruction, if you'd like?"

"You can't destroy that book," says the warlock. "Fire can't burn it. I've tried. Do whatever you want. I'll even give it back to you *after* we help our friend."

"Is it Cadence's book, Alondra's, or yours?" I ask. I turn to the lady. "And what witch are you?"

"Owl-Jay," she says.

"You want to invite your friends to dinner, sweetie?"

"Shut up, Mother!"

"There's no time for this," he snaps. "Give me that book or I'll tear this house to the ground."

"You already teared my house to the ground!"

"Love is something foreign to you, Melanie," says the lady witch. "Out of love, Cadence can save Afreyea. But we need her book, *Broomstick*."

"Love is not foreign to me, dearie. It's foreign to your friend."

"Hand me the book and all this ends, Melanie," the devil says. "I only ask for the book to help Afreyea." He heaves a sigh and says as calmly as he can, "Melanie, I came to help you and your sister. Don't you remember? I didn't possess this house. I first came to help you."

"Liar! You never came for me. You came for Alondra. And you did plenty after, didn't you, warlock?"

I smile. My grin seems to make both witches squirm. I like that. I like to see witches squirm. I have to think of a way to make them squirm some more.

"She's not breathing!" cries the stupid young ewe, that idiot,

young Katie Hassy-horn. I laugh. *"God, she's dying, Melanie! Please! You have to let us help her. Please! Stop casting against her! Please! Give Liam the book!"*

"Shut up!" I cry. I thrust my hand in her direction, and Cadence falls to the ground. "Relinquish your book, relinquish your power." I burst out laughing more. "Your ancestor saved you last time? Who will save you now, my little ewe?"

"Stop it!" cries the lady witch. "Leave Cadence alone!"

"Stop it, Melanie. Stop it! She throwed me down the stairs, Mother! She throwed me down the stairs."

I close my eyes. When I open them, that lady witch looks so serious. And she's come closer. She almost seemed nice before. Now she looks like all them others trying to hurt Momma and me. She waves her hand before my eyes.

"Prohibe," she says.

Does she dare cast a spell on me!?

The devil pulls out a black stick and waves it over my hands.

"Burn," he says. "Burn from the hand that touches what belongs to Hawthorne. Burn by Escoba's ancestor, Cadence's, innocence. Burn the beast's hands that touches her book."

"Burn," the lady echoes with a nod.

I see smoke.

My hands! My hands are burning! My hands are burning, Momma! Oh my god! He's doing it again! They're always hurting us! It's that cursed book. That fiend, that demon from hell, is burning my hands! All he does is hurt us! He's making my skin feel like hot coals, Mother! The cursed book is burning my hands!

"Away with you!" I cry, throwing the book at the devil's face. *"Go away! Stay back from me and my mother and just leave us alone!"*

I slam my door.

~

It's so dark. I can't see anything.

"Momma?"

I don't know where she is. I can't even see my hands. But they're burning. They're hurting so bad.

"They've attacked my home and burned my hands! That devil did it to us again, Momma. They always hurt us!"

And now... it's so dark and... I don't remember the house being this dark. Quiet... and... so dark.

"Are your guests gone? I need help with my brush. It seems it cracked and is dirtier along my back than I—"

"My hands burn!"

19

PRESTO MANIFESTO

Broomstick is back in my hands, and I'm crouching over Afreyea doing everything I can to help her. Her eyes are squeezed tight and she's shaking. Liam and Aunt Jane are standing over me.

"Heal her, Cadence," Aunt Jane says, with a reassuring nod, leaning over me. "Use *Broomstick* to heal her. Touch her and concentrate. With the book, you can heal her."

"But how do you know it will work?"

"It's worked before," Liam says.

I glance back at the house, and that creepy monster, the Samhain Witch, is hunched over by the front door watching me. Her eyes are glowing white in contrast to all her dark, muddy skin. Her whole body is covered in filth. "Mud" indeed. And so creepy. She just keeps staring at me with her white eyes.

I place a hand over Afreyea's chest while clutching my book tightly under my other arm.

"*Cura. Cura. Cura.*"

I don't know what that means—I never know what any of these incantation words mean—but I know it must be magic making me say them.

Afreyea stops shaking. She forces open an eye.

"I'm…okay, Windstorm." Afreyea says. "Enachè nuwe."

Then she turns toward the house and looks at that weird witch staring at us. Mira, Olwyn, and Gala look over at that monster too.

"I don't know how we can finish her destruction," says Olwyn, squinting at her. "She is too powerful, Aurora."

Afreyea nods, breathing heavily. I might have helped her, but she's still really hurt.

"What do you want, Melanie?" I shout, standing up. "What is it you want from us? We'll stop attacking you if you promise to just leave Hawthorne alone!"

Melanie doesn't move. She just keeps staring. Then she shakes her head.

"What is it you want!" I shout, walking closer. I'm pissed. I think seeing another witch hurt, like Kenosha and Agnes, has taken me over the edge.

"Tell me! Why'd you attack me? Why'd you bring out Alondra? The head witches don't want to hurt you, they just want you to leave us all alone! What do you want?"

"Him," she finally croaks, pointing, with an outstretched hand, at Liam.

Liam is rushing toward the house. His eyes appear glassy, as if he's in a trance.

"Tell her what you did, devil," Melanie croaks with a grisly smile. "Unveil to Hassy-Horn what you did to my poor sister. To my family."

"I tried to destroy your hallowed ground."

"*Tried?*" the monster shrieks, shaking her head. "*Tried!* You didn't try. You destroyed it! But everything is my fault, isn't it, witches? *Just like my hand that now burns?* Tell li'l Katie Hass-horn what you did to me. Tell her how my sister, Winnie, died."

"You killed her," Liam says.

"*LIAR.*" Melanie stands up real tall, looking grosser in a

more human form. *"I didn't kill her. You did! You brought the house down on my sister! 'Fess up! Tell the little ewe how you murdered my sister, Winnie, by bringing this house down on her with your magic! Murderer!"*

Liam stops before her at the front door. I'm behind him. He turns and looks almost confused. Then he falls to his knees, clutching his head.

"Liam!" I cry.

He waves a hand at me to stay back. She's hurting him. Just like when my head was in crushing pain when she took me over and killed Agnes.

He crouches down and dips his head in a meditative witch pose. Melanie stands over him, rubbing her right hand over and over—the one he magically burned.

"Abaddon, Abaddon," Melanie taunts slowly. *"Ab-ad-don.* How can you destroy what's already destroyed? What's left to destroy? How can you turn ash into ash when nothing burns? How can you make dust into dust when all has crumbled? Keep your book. I don't need it to take care of you."

Abaddon. Abaddon. Abaddon.

The words aren't said by him, they're whispered around me.

A storm gathers among the trees again, another tempest, this time a spinning wind like a tornado. The wind is uprooting trees in the surrounding forest. Some of the trees are hurled at the house, finally breaking the walls. I believe Liam is casting this, for he's still sitting in a meditative pose, concentrating, under Melanie.

"More, demon!" cries Melanie, goading him to bring more destruction with her hands and bursting into laughter. *"More! Bring it on! Destroy everything! All over again! Who is the Abaddon witch?"*

"You possessed me!" Liam shouts, looking up.

"You took everything from me!" Melanie snarls back. "Now

your wife possesses her successor. Abaddon? All you witches are Abaddon. And I'm going to prove it."

"You took my wife!" Liam shouts, jumping up.

"Liam, stop!" I cry. "You're under her spell!"

"Liam!" warns Jane. "Keep away from her! Cadence, get away from the house! The house is falling."

Liam charges Melanie. He tackles her and throws her against the wall. The impact seems to happen at the same time as the crash of more trees colliding into the house. It's too much for the building. It caves in and half the house comes crashing down.

A rush of dust surrounds me. I cough, batting my hand at the dust. All the while, I still hear Melanie and Liam throwing themselves against walls. And as he wrestles her through the smoke, her thin black snakes are snapping at his face.

"*Come to tear down every last stone!*" screams Melanie. "*Come to take away the evil witch? What is there left of me? Abaddon? Abaddon? I have nothing! But I can take from you.*"

Liam is sucked into the house, as if shot through an airplane window. Then the boarded-up door slams shut before me.

The storm stops.

It's foggy, but there's no rain or wind. Only the noise of a few rocks rolling from collapsed walls can be heard.

It's quiet. Too quiet. After all the wind and destruction, the silence is unsettling.

"Liam!" Jane shouts. She's crying. "No, Lee!"

I rush to the door and try to heave it open, but it won't budge. I run around the side of the house. Although much of the roof has caved in, I don't see any opening. So I run back to the front door and try again to open it.

"Step away, Cadence!" Mira yells.

"Come here, Katie!" Bryce cries. "It's unsafe! Stay back!"

I pull at the door. I can't understand why it's so hard to

open. Is it another one of that bitch's spells? Finally, I throw the door open, but it's pitch black inside, just like on Halloween. I can't see a thing. Nor can I hear anything. Where did Liam and Melanie go?

I turn around. The other witches, including Mira and Bryce, are shouting at me to step away.

"Why'd you come here!" I shout to Aunt Jane.

"Step away from the house," Jane pleads. "Please, Cadence. Please, just step away and I'll tell you."

I walk until I'm a few paces from the door.

"Why! Why are you here?"

"Lee and I came to help you, Cadence," Aunt Jane says.

"But what's happened to him?"

She shakes her head.

"The warlock conjured a spell making the house's walls fall years ago," Gala says. She is crouched over Afreyea. "He killed Winona. She was just a young girl. He didn't mean to. Now the council sees the witch's plan. She used you to lure him here and trap him."

"Then we have to get him out!"

I look at Mira and she nods hesitantly.

"Cadence," Bryce shouts, "just back away from there! It's not safe."

Bryce is right. Another section of the wall falls about a foot away from where I'm standing. It could have broken my leg.

"Help me get Liam out, Bryce! Come here and help me!"

He shakes his head.

"A trap," Afreyea says weakly. "Another trap."

Gala looks at Afreyea and nods. "Cadence, Alondra is inside you. This is not only a trap for Liam, but for you. Stay away from that house."

"I can't leave him!"

"Come back, please, Cadence," urges Bryce.

"The headmaster of the council is hurt," shouts Olwyn. "We've cast our spells. Nothing can stop her."

"The hell with your council! I need help to save Lee!"

"Come back here first, Cadence," Jane says to me, reaching out. "Please. Let's talk first."

I turn my back on them and approach the door. That's when they go nuts. They're all shouting for me to stay away. Half of me wants to listen, to be honest. I can't see anything in the darkness. But then... I think of Liam. I push forward only to have the door slam shut in my face.

When I turn back, I see the witches casting again, with their arms out. That wasn't Melanie, it was my friends and the other witches.

"Open the door!" I cry, whirling back.

"Only backward magic can save Liam," Olwyn shouts, shaking her head.

"Open the door!"

"Your love can't save him from his dark arts, Cadence," Olwyn adds. "Why do you think he asked you to heal Afreyea? He can't cast good magic. Andromeda and Willow warned you."

"Leave him, Windstorm," urges Gala.

Where's Liam, Cadence? Why won't you help bring my husband out of that house? Hawthorne is in danger and you're running out of time.

Alondra! God, they don't know anything, do they? You were right! Enora was right. The council is stupid. Tell me what to do, teacher.

All will be well with all of you if you cast the following incantation at the threshold of the door.

"Tell it to me," I say, looking down and closing my eyes. "Please, teacher. What can I say to save him?"

Cast this spell. But be warned, Cadence. The council is correct. Only dark magic can save my husband now.

"Blessed be, show me."

I kneel before the door.

"She's casting!" Olwyn cries. "We warn you, Windstorm, the council is too weak to help you!"

It's too late. But Alondra does not speak in my mind, she speaks from my lips. I raise my book before the doorway and say, "*Turn your back on me, I still am. Be it virgin or harlot, I remain. From the seed of man art thou. That is all—*"

"Stop!" Gala cries. "Cadence, please, the council warns you!"

"Don't listen to us?" Afreyea asks, weakly. "Maybe listen to a friend?"

~

"Do you remember how Alondra and Reardon initiated me?" Mira asks. It's Mira's voice, but it's dark. Am I inside Melanie's house? "He had ceremonial sex with me, Cadence. He anointed me in mandrake, and then we partook in sex magick."

I open my eyes and find that I'm not in Alabama. I recognize Hilltop Bluff at Hawthorne University. It's nightfall. The evening is lit by a central bonfire.

Mira is standing in her dark cloak with her hands tied behind her back by a rope. She is led by two other black-cloaked witches to the bonfire and a circle of black cloaks. Two long wooden planks have been placed on the ground in the shape of an X. I spot a young Bryce beside the planks on one side. Bill Reardon, the asshole I detest more than anyone else in the world, who Enora murdered, is standing on the other side of the wooden boards. The two witches remove Mira's cloak. Mira's naked. Then they untie her from behind and have her lean against the planks. They tie her wrists to the X.

Tears run down Mira's face.

~

I'm standing before Melanie's broken front door again, but now Mira is blocking the entrance. Somehow, she's appeared right in front of me. But when she looks into my eyes, she falls to her knees crying.

"Disobey me?" I ask sternly in Alondra's voice. "Didn't Afreyea just show Cadence your initiation? Stand aside, Hawthorne witch."

"I'll never disobey you, Alondra," Mira says in tears, shaking her head. "*In sanctum e tenebris inferni, igne sacrificii unctus. Lux tenebris.*"

She moves out of the way and rushes back to the others.

I turn my back on all of them again and face the closed door.

Recite the following words, Cadence, to break this illusion once and for all and set my Lee free.

With my book raised aloft, my mouth moves by Alondra's will:

"*Turn your back on me, I still am. Be it virgin or harlot, I remain. From the seed of man art thou. That is all. Do not fall into trickery. To dust you go, to the depths of hell. In such abyss, nothingness shall pass. And there, you find me. When you close your eyes, I shall manifest in front, not behind. Hide no more, Windstorm. In nothingness lies peace. Know this. I offer your sacrifice, your death. Give me your virginity, I shall return your seed, my semen. This offering, this exchange, done in sanctum for centuries, will allow you to end all suffering. In sanctum e tenebris inferni, igne sacrificii unctus. Lux tenebris.*"

The door doesn't open. Another gale rushes over the house, this time a tornado tearing the walls asunder. The explosion throws me to the ground. Then the whole house explodes. Amid the deafening noise, I think I hear my friends cry out my name. Are they worried I'll be hurt? Rocks and glass from walls and windows break apart, like shards of crystal from a mirror, and burst high up into the air, but the pieces scatter away from me. Then the pieces spin in a vortex and are carried over an empty wild grass glade before me. The whirlwind carries every piece farther into the open field. Then it's all hurled straight down into a hole in the wild grass.

The hole closes.

And her haunted house has completely disappeared.

~

"It is done! It is done!"

I hear a loud bell tone. Then another. Bells are tolling deeply like the bells of a church tower. But many other bells are ringing, making a tinny sound. The bells surround me as if being echoed off the trees in the forest, a thousand deafening bells. And then...laughter. Melanie's laughing again.

Not only is her house gone, every sign of it has disappeared. All that's left is an empty field of bushes and dead trees, spreading out for a mile or so, with scattered tree trunks and weeds. I think this is the house's backyard, previously not visible behind the broken structure. And yet many of the surrounding trees have been uprooted by Mira's and the three head witches' magic. But the house is gone. Not even its foundation remains.

I shudder. Was the house ever even here? If Melanie built the house with a magic illusion, did it exist when we were inside it on Halloween?

"Behold the lamb becomes the bull! The virgin becomes the harlot. We have our sacrifice! We have our soul sacrifice, Momma!"

In the center of the field of dead grass, surrounded by a circle of purple candles, Melanie sits cross-legged, Melanie, a mound of mud, with her head lowered over her filthy naked body. This is a witch conjuring pose. Behind her is an old woman with long white hair, naked and covered in filth and muck, slowly walking aimlessly, back and forth, with her arms out. Her mother, Kathy?

Liam is crouched on his knees on the dirt before me, weeping. I get on my knees beside him. He gropes for me, desperately trying to hold me in his arms.

"Allie," Liam says, crying, taking me into his arms in a tight embrace. "Oh Allie, I'm sorry for what I did. I'm so sorry. I didn't mean for the house to fall on her. I didn't. Do you forgive me?"

"Manifest forgotten and lost sinners!" cackles Melanie's voice, echoing from the woods. *"Arise and spring forth to sprout filth. Witness the defilement of the innocent by the green devil and three-faced monster. Evil grows forth in all witches upon thy sacrifice under Hecate. The evil is you! It's always been you, little ewe! You wicked witch!"*

20

COOKIES

"Care for a cookie, dear?" Aunt Jane asks with a smile, crouching over me. She's holding a tray of large pink sugar cookies with easter eggs frosted on them that she just baked. "They're very good. I find that cookies always help my mood."

I shake my head. Then I glance at Maddie. Maddie flashes a wry grin.

Yep, we're back at Maddie's house staring at walls again. Liam is standing outside by the sliding door, staring at the backyard, with one hand in his pocket and another holding his cellphone. My brother is sitting on the couch across from me, next to Maddie. (Thank god they didn't accompany us this time.)

Can you feel how tense it is? Didn't we already do this when Agnes passed?

"They're really good," says Jane, still hovering over me. "I find that baking helps me when I'm in bad spirits, Cadence. Eating them helps too."

God. No.

God, yes. Did I just sell my soul to the devil?

Maddie shakes her head at her mom, hinting to leave me

alone. But then Aunt Jane shrugs and offers one to my brother. Damie takes three. He lays them on his lap.

Bryce walks into the living room, taps my knee, and sits beside me, showing a rueful grin. I lean my head on his shoulder.

And we sit like this. For, like, forever...

Until a phone rings. It's Liam's cellphone outside. Is it one of his patients? He keeps talking to patients, working. Or could it be one of our witches calling him?

Mira stayed in Alabama with the other head witches of the "council" to watch over Afreyea. Yeah, a witch was sick enough to be seen by a doctor again. But at least this time Afreyea was well enough to say goodbye before we left.

I walk outside. Liam's taken off his Yankee cap and is running his hand through his hair while holding the phone and talking about hospital stuff. He nods at me.

"It's Mira," he says, handing me his phone. "She wants to talk to you."

"Hi, Katie," Mira says on the line. She sounds exhausted.

"God, how is she?"

"*Afreyea is* fine. I'm fine too, by the way, thanks for asking. The doctors are discharging her today. That means the three of them are heading back home. They're not saying goodbye in Hawthorne, they'd rather just fly home from Tallahassee. But that means I'm going to head out with them back home to Orlando."

"What about your stuff?"

"Keep it. It's just a travel bag. I don't have much except a few shirts and pants. You can keep it for next time. Don't worry." She laughs. "Something tells me I'll be visiting Hawthorne again. You can give it back to me when I return. But I want to thank you and Bryce for having me."

"Are you kidding? Thanks for coming, Mira."

"Yeah. I just couldn't miss your transformation."

There's silence.

"That was meant as a joke, Cadence," she says with a chuckle. "Are you still worried about becoming evil? You'll never be evil. Melanie and her mother are just totally nuts. Nothing happened except us getting out of her psycho lair."

"If you say so, Mira."

"I know so. Cadence, you'll always be a Little Bo Peep in my eyes. I just haven't called you that in a long time because I didn't want a windstorm to ignite into a firestorm. If it'll make you feel better, you'll always be a Little Bo Peep in my eyes."

I laugh.

"It was good seeing you. Take care of our coven, will you? And that gem of a husband of yours."

"Sure, Mira. Bye."

"Bye, Cadence. Blessed be."

I hand the phone back to Liam.

"She's going home with the other witches," I say.

"I have to head home too," he says with a nod.

But then he looks awkward, stuffing his hands into his pockets, staring at a rose bush. I think he wants to say goodbye. His awkwardness reminds me of me. Or maybe he's uncomfortable because of what happened last time we were out here. Remember? I tried to jump his bones. Yeah, I mean, we're both pretty weirded out about that. Then there was me casting a satanic witch spell to save him from Melanie's house—which turned out to be a total illusion. Which was pretty fucking weird too. So...do I have to say anything?

To make things weirder, Melanie and her mom completely disappeared after the house shattered.

"Well, bye then," I finally say.

But he doesn't go. I take a deep breath of Aunt Jane's garden: the pleasant smell of jasmine and sage. I look up at the azure sky. There are only a few wisps of white clouds. The weather before Litha is perfect. Aunt Jane's backyard is perfect. But I don't feel perfect.

"Looks like I'm a devil, just like you, I suppose."

"Saying a left-handed incantation doesn't make you a devil, Cadence."

"It does. We've gone through this already. I also killed a sweet old lady, remember? Guess we're quite a pair."

He nods.

"The whole way back Aunt Jane kept telling me that same thing. So did Bryce. Everyone is trying to convince me that I didn't sell my soul to the devil. But the words Alondra had me recite were recited, through black magic, by that sick pervert Bill Reardon in sex ceremonies. I remember. I didn't *do* anything evil. I *said* evil. I recited a sex magic incantation. Isn't that the same thing?"

"Cadence," he says, shaking his head. But he suddenly looks awful talking about this. "I can only wield dark magic now. That's why Alondra's spirit had you cast that black magic spell to save me. I needed your help to finish the witch's destruction. I can't do what you can with white light. That's why I swore to stop practicing. Your final spell made all of our spells—mine, Mira's, your husband's, and the three head witches—work to cleanse those grounds."

"Whatever," I say. shaking my head. "Sure."

Anyway, I can tell he doesn't want to talk about it. I don't want to talk about it either. I honestly think he hates being a witch as much as I do. What a pair, indeed.

"But why'd you come back? You never told me. I was surprised enough when you came back for Agnes, but then you returned to cast magic again after you swore to never do it... Why'd you do that?"

"I already told you. Don't you remember what I said about Alondra being your mother? If Alondra was your mother, what do you think that makes me? If things hadn't turned sour and

Alondra and I had stayed together, you, a witch, would have been not only Alondra's successor, but our daughter. I told you she loved you. We would have loved you together. So? Why ask why Jane and I went there to help you?"

"But you swore to never cast spells again."

"And you never wanted to cast dark magic. But you did. For me. Sometimes we do whatever we need to do, black magic or white, out of love, Cadence. If it's out of love, isn't that good? And I do love my new daughter."

And that feels real good. For the first time, I feel good inside again. He's done it again.

"Hey," he says, backing up and squinting, "you're not going to ruin this by throwing your arms around me again, are you?"

I shake my head and laugh. But I do put my arms out.

"How about a goodbye hug as friends?" I ask.

"I'm glad you came back," I say quietly, hugging him. "Bye."

"Why do you sound so sad?"

"Nothing's changed. Melanie and Kathy can still pester us in Hawthorne."

"I told you she was weakened with the destruction of her hallowed grounds," he says. "She's wandering permanently now."

"I'm not so sure. I'm not even sure if the house was ever standing. The grounds looked empty after her house was destroyed. I'm thinking Melanie conjured the whole thing as an illusion."

"Maybe," he says. "But maybe that conjuring was what we had to weaken. Whether corporeal or incorporeal, I believe destroying her house was worth it. So do the triumvirate of witches."

"But how can you go now? I don't even know if it's safe to hold ceremony?"

"Don't until Kenosha is better. Cadence, I have to leave. I

have a wife and a daughter back home. And a job. I can't stay here. I spoke with the council. They believe you're safe now."

I nod, but I must look terrible, because he puts his hand on my shoulder and frowns.

"How 'bout this. I promise I'll answer my phone next time."

I laugh.

"Bye, Cadence. Your father and Alondra are right about you. So was my vision. You're good for Hawthorne. You might not like being a witch, but I think you make a great one. I think you're a better Hawthorne witch than my wife."

And he heads to the door.

"Wait, Liam, what about your wife? At least tell me how to get rid of her. I can't keep having Alondra popping up. Not just with you...with anyone. It's driving me and Bryce crazy. Agnes and Kenosha met with my coven just to get her to leave. How do I get her to go? Should I perform a ceremony again?"

He looks down in thought for a second. Then he chuckles and shakes his head. "Why don't you just ask Allie to leave? You loved and hated each other enough. Tell her to go away."

"How?"

"Scry, Cadence. Scry."

Scry? What the hell does that mean?

He touches the handle of the sliding door but hesitates before sliding it open. With his back still to me, he says quietly, "Can you tell Allie something? Tell her I love her. Tell her I miss her. I'll always love her. Tell her I'm so sorry that things didn't work out between us. I miss her so much."

"She misses you too."

He slowly nods. Then he smiles and says, "Thanks for saving me, Cadence."

21

JOAN

A PICTURE OF A WOMAN IN MEDIEVAL ARMOR POPS UP BEHIND ME as I stand at the center of the lecture hall stage. The auditorium is packed, as usual.

"You've all heard of Jeanne d'Arc? Or *Joan* of Arc? Let's talk about her. First off, she was called 'd'Arc' after she died. And in France, she was known as Jeanne. I recommend lots of reading on this topic. It will not only give you insight into this amazing historical figure, it will help you better understand the Middle Ages.

"The thing to know, guys, is that Joan lived in a very turbulent time. The Hundred Years' War began in 1337 and ended in 1453. Joan led an army during this war, in 1429. Who was fighting this war? England and France. And France was not doing well when Joan was alive. Here's a map." I click a button on my remote and a map of France and England shows up behind me. "France was fractured by a civil war with followers of the Duke of Burgundy, Burgundians, aligning with England, and Joan supported the Armagnac, following King Charles VII. Look on the map behind me. As you can imagine, England was licking its chops over a final conquest, until Joan came along to save their country.

"But this hero was a bit odd, wasn't she? For one thing, she was a *she*. And this was not a time when women wore men's clothing. If I had lived back then, I wouldn't have been permitted to wear slacks." I slap my leg. "Look here at this famous painting." I press the slide button. "Joan is kissing a sword and looking up. The reason for the sword is obvious. She was a general. Why is this general looking up? Joan claimed that she was sent by the angel Michael to fight for God, while the English claimed she was a witch. But what do you think happened back then to women wearing slacks like mine?"

I press another button and it's gory. This is one of the slides that Kenosha spoke of during my botched lecture: of a person being burned alive—probably not tame enough for the lecture hall, but classic Alondra. And the students are loving it.

"Remember when Doctor Trent spoke of heresy and burning witches? Well, after Joan lost favor and she was tried by the English, they burned her alive. But wearing pants wasn't the only thing that condemned her. It was her claim that she was receiving visions."

I change the grisly slide, preferring a picture of Joan in armor, riding with her army.

"So...could this be the first documented burning of a witch? Some contend the first documented case had happened ten years earlier. But certainly, this would be the earliest well-known case. To the English, Joan of Arc was a witch. Was she? Or was she sent by God?

"People claim Joan had many mysterious powers. Joan prayed before a stillborn child, and the child was revived. Another time, a soldier claimed that she ordered him to step aside. A moment later, a soldier who had taken his place was killed by cannon fire. Joan was a brilliant strategist, able to defeat generals far more seasoned and experienced."

I hit a button and only a yellow light shines behind me.

"A few weeks ago, I asked you all to write an essay on evil. On one side, Joan of Arc represented a messenger of God, but on the other, she was a devil, able to defeat whole armies by selling her soul. Which one was she? A messenger of god or a devil witch? With the permission of our professor, Dr. Wallace..." I look down. My hubby nods excitedly. He's smiling over another triumphant lecture by yours truly. "This will be your assignment. Do you love Joan of Arc? If so, tell me why. Do you hate her? Was she evil for wearing men's clothes?" I touch my slacks again. Some students laugh. "Write about it."

"Another great lecture by Mrs. Wallace," Bryce hollers, rushing up the steps and clapping. "Way to go, Cadence," he says quietly, covering my mic.

"Love ya," I say in his ear.

"Let's do that, shall we?" Bryce rearranges his computer on the podium. "Let's write about Joan of Arc, just as Mrs. Wallace suggests. You guys have two weeks to complete the essay. And now, I'm going to switch over to some more housekeeping items. A multiple choice quiz on the bubonic plague is set for next Wednesday. And—"

I make my way up the side aisle to leave early. A few students nod and smile. Yeah, they totally love me now.

Then I open the door and squint as bright sunlight rushes into my eyes. It's hot with clear skies. I check my cellphone. 10:30. I'm already late, but I really wanted to do that talk for the class.

I cross the quad, making my way to the parking lot. Then I get into Alondra's dark gray Jaguar. I guess Alondra's old car is mine now. I said Mr. Hanley could have it, but he said it goes better with the house. I hardly mind. It's beautiful. Bryce and I had it just sitting in the garage for the longest time. Now I'm off for a quick drive to the student houses surrounding our school.

The phone rings on my speakers, unfortunately interrupting the awesome guitar solo from the Smashing Pumpkins song "That's the Way."

"Hey, babe," says Maddie. "Where are you?"

"I'm coming over now."

"How'd it go?"

"I killed it."

"That's two for two, Cadence. Alondra always knew you could do it if you just got out of your shell."

"It's one for two. The first lecture was a total disaster, remember, Madds?"

"Whatever. No one thought that but you."

"I'll be there in a minute, 'kay?"

"Well, sorry, but I'm heading out. Damie and I really want to head to Atlanta to go shopping this morning. I promised him. I just made a quick visit."

"Oh, sorry I missed you."

"It's not like you won't see me tonight, Katie."

"What's tonight?"

"It's Friday, dope. Our sabbath."

"Oh, yeah."

"Sometimes you're as absent minded as your brother."

"You sure it's safe?"

"You tell me, High Priestess."

"Okay. I'll ask her when I get there. Bye, Maddie."

"Bye. And congratulations."

I arrive at a really small old white house next to a hundred others in a neighborhood close to campus. This is a nice area. Had I not fallen in love with you-know-who, I could have seen myself living here after the dormitories. Then I look behind me at the back seats and curse. I forgot the flowers. Shit! They're still sitting on the island in my kitchen back home.

Maybe Maddie's right. Maybe I am getting as absent minded as Damien?

After a deep breath, I get out and make my way up a few

steps to the front door. Then I knock. An older dark-skinned woman wearing glasses answers the door.

"I'm Cadence."

"Come in, Cadence," the lady says with a smile.

"Shirl, I'm going to need a goddamn bath, okay," says someone inside. "You think you can get that ready for your invalid sister?"

"She's such a pain in the ass," Shirl says to me, shaking her head and rolling her eyes.

"I heard that? Who's here now? I thought Madison just left?"

Shirl just shakes her head again and smiles.

I take off my shades and look around. The house is small and simple. The walls are painted dark red, almost brown. I think her home only has two rooms, almost like a studio apartment. There's a living room at the entrance, a small washer-and-dryer room and, I'm guessing, her bedroom. It smells like incense. That smells nice. The floor is tinny and creaky, making noise with my every step. In the living room is a very small area for an oven, stove, and table. I suppose that's the kitchen. And on the living room walls are pictures that appear to be of the African continent. I see ladies in headdresses, some ritual masks, and a lovely landscape painting. Of course, there's a very large wooden pentagram over a fireplace. Beside the pentagram is a metal cross. There's no TV that I can see.

"Come in," Shirl says. "Grouch is in the bedroom."

The master bedroom is simple, with just a bed and bookcase, but the bookcase is overflowing with books. In fact, there are also boxes full of books. Aside from the books, the room seems empty enough to be moved into. A bit farther down the hall, I spot a door with a window. There's no backyard. The back door opens into our open forest. I love that. When you think of it, even though this home is so simple, this is something Alondra would love. Alondra was all about her library of books upstairs and her backyard opening to the woods. Only she was more uppity about everything—like my car.

"Hi, Cadence," Kenosha says, waving and scooting up a little in bed. She's bald, in blue pajamas. There's a hint of a smile. "Shirl, can you get the chair from the other room again?"

"Sure, okay," Shirl says.

Kenosha cups her hand and says quietly, "My sister thinks I slave-drive her. Isn't that funny?"

Hmm, sounds familiar.

Shirl comes back with a wooden chair, and I plop down beside Kenosha's bed. She sits up even more.

"You just missed Madison."

"I know."

"So, how are you holding up?"

"No different from usual in this crazy, weird town, I suppose," I say, heaving a sigh. Then I lose my smile. "It's been difficult."

She reaches for my hand. I give it to her.

"How are you, Kenosha? Are you feeling better? I would have visited you in the hospital—"

"Seems you and Mira had enough going on."

"You heard about Alabama?"

"I told the triumvirate not to go. But no one ever listens to me, do they?" She pauses. She puts up a finger and closes her eyes tightly for a moment. I think she's in pain. "I can't get worked up. I just had heart surgery."

"I heard. We've been so worried about you."

"Yeah, well, I'm all right. I told the doctors that it was caused by stress from running the college. If they only knew."

"I'm so sorry, Kenosha," I blurt out. "I didn't mean to hurt you. I've been so worried ever since that night. I've felt so—"

"I know, Cadence. You did hurt me. But that's okay, because you know what? You're the only one who listened to me." Then she bursts out laughing real hard. I don't know why it's so funny. "I asked you to hold that ceremony, remember? You're the only one who listens." She's still guffawing. I take my hand back and feel a little uncomfortable. Then I force a smile. I mean, I love the fact that she seems happy. "I'm the senior witch in Hawthorne. Why apologize? It was my fault."

That irks me a bit. This witch is so pompous that she's taking responsibility for my hex that led to her heart attack. Well, I guess if she doesn't want to blame *me*—

"We fight too much, Cadence," she says, turning serious and taking my hand and patting it. "You know that? Do you know why?"

I shake my head. She squeezes my fingers.

"You act like Alondra."

I snatch my hand back. I don't like that at all.

"You didn't get along with her either."

"Yes, but when Alondra grew older, we understood each other, we respected each other, and we cared for one another. I asked Madison to meet tonight in ceremony. Of course, I can't make it. But I think you should meet with your friends. You've done well with your coven. Your sisters listen to you, and they care for one another."

"Is it safe?"

"For now. Yes. I think you should do it."

"Did you hear what I had to do to save Liam?"

"Olwyn told me."

"What do I do now?"

"It was a left-handed spell. Every one of us has free choice, in the arts, to choose the right or the left." Then she turns and winces. "Fuck, this pain. You know what chest pain and the inability to breathe teaches me, Cadence?" She grabs my hand and squeezes it hard again. "This. Stop it, okay? Let's just stop it, Cadence. All right?"

I nod, but I don't know what the hell she's talking about. Is she talking about fighting? Or is she talking about pain? Or is she talking about caring about the pain? Or is she talking about all of it? I don't know.

She just squeezes my fingers and smiles. Then she shakes a finger and closes her eyes again.

"I have that stupid imbecile Dr. Bainer running Hawthorne in my stead right now," she says. "God help us, right? I mean Dr. *Brainer*."

I laugh. I thought only the students knew that nickname.

"Cadence, I'm hard on you and Bryce because I'm hard on myself. I want you to be as good as Alondra. Your teacher drove me totally nuts, but I respected her more than any witch I've ever known. I loved Alondra, Cadence. I've told you this again and again, but you never seem to believe me. I loved her. And she told me so many times that she loved you."

"She rarely mentioned you."

"Because you and she had the same relationship we do. But it took me being near death to see how I've failed you. Andromeda understood. Agnes was right about everything."

But then she stops talking, closing her eyes tightly again. She starts breathing heavily.

After she doesn't talk for a long time, it starts freaking me out. She's just breathing heavily with her eyes closed.

"Are you all right, Kenosha?" I ask, jumping up. "Where does it hurt?"

She points to her chest, squeezing her eyes. I take my hand from hers and press lightly on her chest. I don't know why, but somehow I don't feel like it's a whole lot different from touching her hand. With her inspiration and expiration, I follow her chest with my hand. Weirdly, it's reminding me of when I touched the deer in my recent wandering trance. That sends a flood of memories of the doe's soft fur. I loved the animal's fur. But was it the fur or was it this closeness? No...maybe it was the pleasure of feeling the deer's energy. Black magic takes life or spirit in sacrifice. Does white magic celebrate it?

When I open my eyes, Kenosha is staring wide-eyed at me.

"How'd you do that?" She scoots up in bed.

"Do what?"

"Get rid of my pain? How? By just touching my chest? How did you do that, Cadence?"

I shrug.

"Is Alondra really inside you, Cadence? Not just some ghost or spirit, but is Allie actually there? Is Allie really inside you?"

She stares into my eyes. I'm fearing that they will turn green.

"I don't want her to be there anymore, Kenosha."

"Can you tell her I'm sorry? I'm sorry that we weren't closer. I thought when she invited me to campus it would finally heal our past. It didn't, Cadence. It's true, we loved each other, but we were still so distant."

"I know, Willow." And that voice was Alondra's.

"What?" Kenosha asks. She scoots up again in bed. "Cadence, I mean, Alondra... Alondra, tell me, what can I do to save the college? Save the town? How can I shield us from harm? How can I fix what we've already done? How can I protect your sisters and Cadence?"

"Save Melanie."

I drop her hand, turn from her, and jump up.

I feel sick. I'm so unsteady. So dizzy. I feel like throwing up. I feel a rush of crushing pain in the middle of my chest.

"Shirl! Shirl!"

Kenosha's room is spinning. The walls are moving so fast around me, as if I'm spinning. I feel like I'm going to vomit. I can't focus. Then something, or someone, helps me back to the chair.

"Ow," I say. "Ow!" I'm clutching my chest. The pressure hurts so bad! "Ow. Ow!"

"What's happening, Kenosha?" asks Shirl in a panic.

"She transferred my pain to her, I think," says Kenosha.

"Are you all right, Cadence?" asks Shirl. "Should I call the doctor?"

The pain recedes, but I still feel sick. God, is this what Kenosha felt when I walked in? It was so much pain. So sick. So horrible. And all because of me. No, not my spell, Alondra, *your* spell.

"I don't want her inside of me anymore, Kenosha! Why is she still here? I love her, but I want her to leave. I want her to come out of me!"

Kenosha doesn't answer.

I turn and see Shirl crouched on a knee beside me, looking worried.

"You okay, Cadence?" asks Shirl.

I nod. I force a smile and say, "I'm fine. It's passing."

"I'm just in the other room, okay?" Shirl says, getting up.

After more silence, with Kenosha and me alone in the room, I ask quietly, "What's New Orleans like? I've never been." I know it sounds real weird and random, but I never asked Kenosha about her home. And I want to do anything I can to get my mind off the pain.

"Your ancestor, Escoba, lived there. Well, I love the food, Cadence. And the buildings in the French Quarter are so different and fun for visitors. But the grounds around the city are what I love the most. The trees. The moss from some of the trees dips down, under bright moonlight, into the water. My coven is in the forest, like here, where the trees are numerous, but not thin, more like large trunks with branches drooping near ponds and streams. It's more like the trees west of here, like in Savannah. The trees are so beautiful."

"You miss it?"

"Yes," Kenosha says with a nod. "I do. But I miss my sisters more. Sometimes, on rare occasions, witches from my coven still visit."

"You gave up all that for me?"

"No. I've devoted my life to the arts. I came to Hawthorne for witchcraft, not you. Alondra and I waited for someone with as much psychic energy as you, even before Liam predicted your arrival."

"How was your lecture this morning?" Kenosha asks.

"You knew I lectured?"

"Yes. I thought it was odd that you wanted to meet at this time."

"I wanted to see you as soon as I heard you were back."

"You're feeling better?" she asks.

I nod. The pain is completely gone.

"What did you lecture about, Cadence? *Evil?*" She infernally smirks. But then she winks.

"Joan of Arc."

"Same thing," she says, rolling her eyes.

"How is that the same thing, Kenosha?"

"You chose Joan of Arc for her being accused as a witch, right? Why else would you choose that topic? Was she a witch, as the English claimed, or was she working by divine intervention? Was she a devil or divine? Evil or good? Wasn't that the basis of your lecture?"

I nod.

"And it went well, didn't it? I expect no less from my prized graduate student. You know, Cadence, you and Bryce are under the same stress as I am. We have to carry Alondra's metaphysical class on our shoulders. Just like you have to carry on her Hawthorne coven. I mean, you even live in her house. We all have to continue her legacy. That is how great your teacher was. And that makes it stressful for all of us."

"I think I was asking you about New Orleans to get your mind off all of it, Kenosha. Don't forget she's a little too close to me right now."

She pauses and puts a finger up again, closing her eyes.

"Are you in pain again?"

"No, it's just a habit. I thought it might be pain because my heart was beating faster."

"I wish you could have gone to Alabama with us."

"Melanie would have killed me. The three witches that went with you weren't directly responsible for what happened to Liam and those grounds. Agnes and I were. She killed Agnes. Melanie used Alondra's magic inside you, but Alondra didn't kill Agnes. Neither did you. Melanie acted through you."

"I don't even know what happened. I blacked out."

"But *you* didn't, did you, *Allie*? No, I think you made plenty of mistakes, Alondra, but murder was never one of them. I don't think you meant to hurt me." She chuckles. "You don't mind if I talk to Alondra inside of you, do you Cadence?"

"Go right ahead. Maybe it'll get her the hell out."

"Alondra is very stubborn, like you. She'll leave when she feels like it." Kenosha laughs. "Cadence, through our arts back home, the spirit world is very much a part of our daily lives—particularly ancestors. Hoodoo believes in only a very thin veneer between the living and the dead. *Save Melanie?* Huh. That is so Alondra, always surprising me by telling me exactly the opposite of what I'd expect. She was such a pain in the ass, Cadence. And after what she did to my dear friend Andromeda? No, Alondra, no. I have no intentions of saving Melanie."

"Melanie just wanted me to practice left-sided magic, I think, to take my soul."

"Words can't take your soul, Cadence."

I shrug.

"They can't," she repeats with a smirk. "You know, when I was a child, I played with a Ouija board. That's black magic too. It doesn't mean I'm destined for hell. A taste of black magic is not enough to turn you. It's a start, and I don't approve...but you saved my friend Liam, didn't you? And it didn't turn you. *Yet...* But a taste is a start in the wrong direction."

"I hope you're right."

"I'm always right. I'm your dean."

That makes both of us laugh.

"How long will I have to withstand Dr. Brainer?"

"I hope to come back to work in a couple months. But whether it be school or witchcraft trouble, all you have to do is knock on my door. I want you to feel like you can always do that. After all, you know I came here for you. I'm not only here for the coven, I'm also here for you as your dean."

"Medicine time," says Shirl, walking in carrying some bottles. "I take it you're better, Cadence?"

"You make a really good nurse," I say with a nod.

"I am a nurse," Shirl says. "Just never thought I'd have to take time off work at the hospital to help my sister."

"See, we don't like each other either," Kenosha says.

"Oh, you hate her too, Cadence?" Shirl asks, sorting out some meds from a bottle on the nightstand. "Kenosha is not a very likable person."

Shirl hands Kenosha the medicine with a cup of water. Kenosha brings the pills close to her mouth but, before she swallows, she says to both of us, "Thank you. And thanks for visiting me, Cadence."

22

SCRYING

I'M SITTING CROSS-LEGGED ON THE FLOOR IN THE DARK, WITH A single lit candle, facing a large mirror in my guestroom. My book, *Broomstick*, is on my lap. I'm reading a page I probably glanced over a few hundred times in the past, written by Alondra about divination.

Glass has many meanings. It had profound spiritual meaning ever since the Jews fashioned it thousands of years ago in honor of their god's purity. The mirror also denotes vanity, hence the fury of the witch in Snow White over not being the prettiest in the land. But it also carries psychological meaning. Like the deepest meditation, it is gazing within oneself, witches.

Scrying, pronounced "s-crying," has been used by fortune tellers and wizards since ancient times. It is also called "seeing." The practitioner picks a quiet, dark place, uses any reflective object, steadies her breathing, and stares at the reflections within the object. I recommend faint illumination, like a single candle. More advanced witches can use different colored flames, smoke, or even dark, mirrored surfaces, like the classic black mirror, to peer into the unknown. But the reflective object can be anything from the legendary crystal ball of gypsies to the famous mirror of Maria Sophia's evil stepmother ("Snow White" in the Brothers Grimm's fairy tale).

When a medium stares into glass, she is not only unlocking a doorway to another world, she is peering into herself. And so, it is strongly advised that the practitioner carry no disorganized thoughts or fractured ego, and that the practitioner cleanse herself and ensure she is at her highest level of purity before attempting to gaze into the mirror. Otherwise, she will not be gazing at the unlocked occult world, she'll be gazing into her own fractured mind.

∾

Well, Alondra, there goes the whole point of this exercise. I've got quite a fractured mind with you hanging around.

∾

Pick a quiet space where you cannot be disturbed. As in meditation, ensure you are at peace. Like the perfect reflective glass of the mirror, you, the Seer, must reflect thoughts and images within yourself. Keep everything dark. Again, I recommend a single candle flame.

Sit in a lotus position. Observe, and remember, that the lotus position—with shoulders, knees, and head—forms the geometric shape of a pentagram. The area around your base forms a blessed circle encircling the five points. A pentacle. And so, if you are in the correct position, you do not need to create a special circle with chalk or draw a pentagram in the center. This position seen sideways, or in two dimensions, also forms the triangle representing the body in alchemy: sulfur, iron, and mercury. Finally, it forms the trinity in ancient Rosicrucian and Hermetic traditions, representing body, soul, and spirit. Gather up all your energy from this posture. Then center your focus on the surrounding space. If need be, for focus, dip your head down.

After focusing on darkness, witches, stare into the mirror. Think of what you are longing for. Your desire. If you are using a black mirror, you will see only the flickering flame. If it is a ball of glass or flat mirror, you will see yourself. Disregard your own image, but ensure that you can still see a shadow of yourself in the border of the glass. Even in the black mirror, seeing your shadow is helpful. And then, again, focus repeatedly on your desires. If you would like, you may add the ancient Latin words for reveal: Revelare. Revelare. Revelare.

Now go and see that which is hidden, witches. The occult.

But permit me a final warning. This magic is not right-sided. This is dark magic. Your soul does not reside on Earth to see what shouldn't be seen. Practitioners more familiar with black magic may note that the above steps are precisely the same if you wish to summon a demon, only demonic summoning is cast with different intent. If you are a novice or unsure of Hecate's spirit residing in you, close this book and turn away. Do not gaze into the mirror. But if you meet this challenge, prepare to journey into the wonder of the past, present, future, and far off worlds. And scry.

Hmm. Well, I think I have the magical power. I've levitated, thrown an evil witch a hundred yards across a field, and healed Kenosha's chest. But I've been told often enough not to practice dark magic. Still, if this is the only way to ask for you to go away, Alondra...blame your husband. Scrying was his idea to get rid of you.

I sit straighter, throw my long hair back, and look into the mirror before me. I close *Broomstick* but keep it on my lap. Then I close my eyes and meditate on my steady breathing, as my teacher, Alondra, taught me countless times. I take one more deep breath. Then...

I gaze into the mirror.

My face is lit under the flickering yellow flame. It's so dark in my guest room that I can't see anything else. So the area around my profile is just darkness—like a black mirror, I suppose. Although it's late, I left my black mascara and lipstick on. And I see my black nightgown. I mean, I wore black because I'm casting spells, so I wanted to look the part.

I take another deep breath. Then I see my frown. Because this feels stupid.

Okay, deep concentration, right?

I focus on the flickering light by my profile.

"*Revelare,*" I say quietly. "*Revelare magister. Revelare Alondra. Alondra Johansen. Venite foras. Come to me, teacher. Come forth so that you may leave me alone.*"

Nothing. Just a flickering light. But I feel ease. Calm.

I feel magic.

"*Revelare.* Come to me. *Venite foras, Alondra Johansen.*"

I see my profile and the yellow flickering light of my single candle. But when I close my eyes, I see Bryce. That's weird. Our bedroom becomes vivid in my mind. I see him sleeping upstairs in bed. It's very late or...very early. He must have left the dining room and finally gone to bed.

Wait. Shit! I have to keep my eyes open, right?

I stare at the glass again.

My eyes turn toward the reflection of my face. I can't help it. My face is right there. My head slightly moves with every inspiration and expiration. My lips twitch ever so slightly. I see my eyes. Thankfully, they're brown. But perhaps that's why nothing is happening? Maybe I'm too spooked for them to turn green?

The contours of my cheeks and chin start blurring. My focus is on those twitching black lips, open ever so slightly with every slow breath. My eyes are open, but squinting. But even my eyes and forehead are blurring. Everything, even the candle, is blurring into shadows. No...my face is changing. Alondra? Is it you? I wait, breathing in and out ever so slightly.

"*Venite foras. Venite foras. Revelare. Revelare Alondra Reardon.*"

I finally recognize a face in the flickering glass. It's not mine. It's...

Enora!

~

There's a loud shriek. I open my eyes wide and rise to my knees. It's so dark around the mirror in my guest room that I have to grope on the wall for the light switch. It sounded like the yell was coming from upstairs.

"*Get out!*" It's Alondra's voice. "*Get the fuck out of my house! It is one thing in ceremony, quite another in my own home! In my own bed! I never want to see you again. Not only in our circle, but in my home! Get the hell out!*"

"*How is this any different from you?*" cries another voice. This is Enora's, but she sounds like she's crying. "*How is it any different from what you made me do with Bryce in ceremony, teacher!*"

"*You dare open your mouth! I'll shut it for good. I warn you. Get the hell...*"

Alondra's voice fades.

Then it gets so quiet. Too quiet. I still haven't turned on the lights. I stand up. Then I creak open the guest room door. A shadow rushes by my feet. It's not Whiskers. Whiskers is a clumsy fat gray cat. This is a thin black cat. Could a stray have appeared inside the house?

There's still no sound. It's as if the shouting never happened. But I know I heard it upstairs.

I make my way up the stairway.

Revelare. Falconsong. Revelare. Revelare. Alondra Reardon.

Alondra *Reardon*? Why would I think of that name? I think

that's the only time I ever called her by her second husband's name.

There's a crash behind me. It sounds like broken glass. I turn on the stairs, but I see only darkness below. I rush downstairs but see that our main hall is dark too. I turn on a hall light. There's no one here.

I pass the dining room. I glance at the kitchen. Under a few night-lights, there's no sign of any broken glass. The clock on the oven reads three-fifteen. Witching hour or not, I feel really freaked out right now. I feel like my own house is haunted. Is this what left-sided magic does to one's mind? To one's own house?

"*Hypocrite!*" cries Enora. "*How dare you threaten me over black magic, Falconsong! Who taught me this?*"

That makes me rush back upstairs. If Enora's upstairs, she could be attacking Bryce!

"*Get out!*" yells Alondra. "*Get out before I show you real magic, you stupid fucking tramp!*"

The fuss is definitely coming from my bedroom. And now I see the lights are on.

I rush inside.

A very young-looking Enora is standing holding a bedsheet over her naked body, leaning against our floor-to-ceiling window. Alondra is in her professor clothes—the older Alondra I remember well. I've seen her in this dark blouse, pants, and leather jacket, lecturing. But in bed, Bryce isn't lying there, it's Bill Reardon, in a fetal position, covering his crotch with his hands. The old creep is naked. It looks like Enora took all the bedsheets to cover herself.

"You mind if I get my clothes first, *teacher*?" asks Enora sarcastically. Then she shakes. I think it's because Alondra's green eyes are wider than ever.

"We were practicing Thelema from *The Book of Lies*, Falconsong," says Reardon.

"Don't lie to me, Bill. You were fucking her. This isn't a ceremony. You were simply fucking one of my students."

"If you'll calm the hell down," Enora says, "I'll get my clothes and leave."

Alondra's eyes change into a creepy pearly all-white. She raises an arm toward Enora. Enora screams. Her whole body is lifted and dragged along the carpet by her toes. The shock makes her drop her sheet and leaves her naked. A moment later she is hovering in thin air. Then she's thrown forward until she falls into Alondra's grasp. With Enora's body still hovering over the floor, Alondra starts choking her with one hand.

Bill Reardon jumps out of bed.

"Stop this!" Reardon says. "This is all my fault, Alondra! Let her go. Just leave her be."

"Everything is your fault, Bill!" Alondra cries. "Our whole coven has fallen to ruin because of you!"

Someone rushes into the room behind me. I'm shocked to recognize my husband. But my husband is so young. He's wearing preppy clothes, and he looks like a little boy.

"Disciple," Reardon says, shaking his head. "Leave the room now."

"What's going on, Alondra?" Bryce asks. "What is she doing here!"

"Are you going to choke me to death, teacher?" asks Enora between gasps. Alondra is still holding her up with one hand, choking her. Enora's kicking her toes in the air, trying to contact the carpet to stand. "Huh? Kill me? Who is the one practicing black magic now?"

Alondra looks at Bryce. She loses her scowl. Then her wrathful expression fades, and she looks terribly sad.

Enora's body drops to the ground.

"Get out," Alondra says quietly with a broken voice. "Get out. Both of you. Get out of my house."

"It was a ceremony, I tell you, Alondra," Reardon says. "It was just Thelemic sex magic. We were trying—"

"Shut up, Bill. Leave me alone and get out of my house."

Enora walks over to a chair and throws a black dress over her head. Reardon runs to a dresser and throws on his pants and a shirt.

"All you do is hurt people," Bryce snaps at Enora as she walks by him.

She doesn't respond to him. They both rush out.

Then Alondra and Bryce stand over her bed staring at it. I'm standing beside them. And after the front door opens and slams shut, Alondra falls to her mattress with her head in her hands, weeping. I've never even seen Alondra cry before. Standing over her, watching her tears, I cry too. I remember hearing about this affair from Bryce once, but he never told me he witnessed it in person. At first, Bryce just stands over Alondra watching her cry, but then he gently sits beside her on the bed. He puts an arm around her.

"Oh, Bryce, stay with me tonight," Alondra says. "I just need someone in the house. Just stay over in the guest room. Can you?"

"Okay."

"Did you know about this?" Alondra asks, wiping her nose with the back of her hand. "How long has this been going on outside of ceremony?"

Bryce doesn't answer.

"It hurts so much," Alondra says. "God. I want to hurt her back. God, I wanted to kill Enora, Bryce. I think I could have. I could have easily strangled her to death. And I don't, I don't know if I care anymore." She moves away from him. "Stay away from Bill, okay? Just stay away from him. No more lessons. I don't want him anywhere near you ever again."

"Okay," Bryce says.

"I don't want him poisoning you, Bryce. Okay? You're pure."

"Okay."

But then she just keeps crying. And Bryce just sits there quietly beside her for support.

"What is this pain?" she asks, brushing tears from her eyes. "It's the worst pain, worse than any wound I've ever felt. It's like..." She looks up, oddly pensive, as tears streak down her cheeks. "It's like Jesus on the cross, Bryce. Jesus's last words were 'Why have you forsaken me?' I never understood those final words. I never could understand what he meant. Of all words, why were those his last? Now I get it. I finally understand. Whipped, thrashed, and bled by the scourge and then nailed to a cross, but that wasn't his greatest torture. The greatest torture of all in Jesus's life was not physical pain, but losing the one he loved—losing God. That was his ultimate final sacrifice for us. His loss of God. But, Bryce, I am no god or prophet, I am damned. I have no resurrection for God to return to me. Nothing to put me at ease. All I feel is darkness and pain."

"You have the sisters in our circle. Our friends. And you have me."

"I've failed this life." She shakes her head vehemently. "That is why I can only hope for another."

Then she looks up and those green eyes gaze right into mine. I lurch back and feel totally creeped out. Because she can see me. She's staring right at me. Her eyes are still moist, but she clearly sees me. And it's like the Alondra I saw in the coffee house. This is not a ghost. Alondra, my teacher, is sitting under me.

"Windstorm. This I breathe. Hawthorne Witch. Wait for the next one. And leave me, Cadence. It's me. It's me."

But as sad as she was, she said those words without emotion.

"I don't understand why you keep saying that to me, Alondra," I cry, shaking my head. "Alondra, I summoned you in the mirror to ask you to leave me alone. I can't keep being possessed by you."

"Do not scry, Cadence," Alondra says calmly. "I promised to reveal to you everything. Don't you see what I unveiled? Liam took Melanie. Bill took Enora. Save them. I couldn't save them in my last days. Save Melanie and Enora." She looks down, now more meditative than sad, and says with a sly grin, "I promise to leave afterward. But when I go...won't you miss me, daughter?"

I see my face in the mirror beside a flickering candle. I've been sitting in the guest room before the glass all along. And now, in dim light, I see my vision's over. But tears still fall from my eyes.

23

OSTARA EGGS

I wake up in bed to knocking on the door downstairs. It's early morning. I can tell from all the yellow light shining through our huge bedroom window, making me squint. Bryce stirs. Mr. Handsome is sleeping beside me.

"Who can that be now?" he grumbles.

"Don't know."

"What time is it, babe?" Bryce asks, stretching and yawning.

"Morning."

I stretch and get out of bed. Then I shuffle real slowly, in my black nightgown, down the stairway. There's more rapping against the door. It reminds me of the last time someone knocked. That was the three witches. I really hope it isn't them again.

"Just a second," I mumble.

I reach the door. I look through our peep hole and then feel creeped out. All I see is our driveway, our red decorative carriage, blue sky with a few wisps of white clouds, and tons of trees. There's no one there.

"Who is it?" asks Bryce. He's standing right behind me in his blue robe.

I shrug. I unlock and open the door.

It's really pleasant outside. A nice day for Ostara. Flowers are finally growing in our front yard. I have lilies and other flowers, and I've started tending to the front yard as a garden. Maddie's mom gave me the idea. Alondra always had a lovely garden in front of the house. So I figured I'd try my hand at gardening and replant it. You know, maybe I won't hate being a witch if I become a green one?

In our long driveway, I don't see any other cars. Only our decorative red carriage and our two old luxury cars parked beside the house.

"Weird. Maybe it's some kids playing a prank?"

"No, Cadence," Bryce says, pointing to the ground. "Look down."

A black bird is fluttering on the ground, struggling to move. It's dragging its body on one side. It seems to have a broken wing, and there are bloody scrapes along its side. There's also blood all over its chest and stomach.

"Ew, gross."

Bryce quickly shuts the door.

"Are we gonna just leave it outside like that?"

"Yes," Bryce says. "That's exactly what I'm going to do."

"You do realize the raven is Enora's totem?"

"It could just be a bird that was some animal's prey," he replies, shaking his head. "There are plenty of black birds around, Cadence. Come on." And he takes my hand and leads me to the kitchen. "Today's special. Remember? Let's not think about spells, witchcraft, magic, or anything else this morning. In fact, how about we forget 'bout witchcraft? It's our anniversary. I'll sweep the bird from our porch later." He yawns. "You want to join me for breakfast? Or go back upstairs and sleep longer?"

"Join you, lover." And I reach up on my tippy toes, brushing his hair with my fingers and touching my lips to his. "Happy anniversary."

I run my hand along his head as we make out, then I massage his back. He brings me close. We just enjoy making out. And it's wonderful.

"How about I make some eggs as a celebration, *Mrs. Wallace.* We'll have a nice anniversary breakfast?"

"I'd love that. But aren't you already planning to take me somewhere for dinner too? Just don't tell me it's Lacey's."

"Yep, got a reservation at Lacey's."

"Bryce," I say, rolling my eyes.

"It's the best steak in town, Katie."

"Happy anniversary, darling," I say with a laugh. "I love you so much. You're pure, you know that?"

"Pure," he says between kisses. "Hmm, Alondra used to call me pure. I think she called you that too."

"Really? Sunny side up for me, okay?" I step back. "Not yucky, runny scrambled like you like. Remember it had blood that time? I'm totally traumatized by that. That was so gross."

"Okay," he says. "But I'll risk the blood. I hate sunny side up."

"Love you."

But I really don't know when he'll get around to actually making us eggs. We're too busy smooching.

We're about halfway through our anniversary breakfast, on our small kitchen table, when there's another knock. And this one is in a pattern, like a person, not like the last time. I think that freaks me out more because I'm thinking about the bird turning into Enora again. We just stare at each other with wide eyes.

"My turn," he says, sliding back his wooden chair and getting up.

"No, Bryce." There's a knock again. "I'll get it."

We head to the door together. I look through the peep hole again. Then I heave a sigh. It's not Enora. It's a couple. But I don't know who these people are.

I open the door.

A pale guy with short, dark facial hair in a blue beanie is standing beside a thin blond girl with a white sweater. They're holding hands. I check their feet, and thankfully the injured black bird is gone. They really couldn't look any more normal.

"Is the Hawthorne Witch here?" the young woman asks. She has a thick southern accent. "Alondra Billington?"

"I'm Cadence. Alondra isn't here anymore."

The guy looks down for a moment, removing his hat. He glances at the blond lady. His wife? She nods.

"A man named Raymond checked out our home a few years ago," the stranger says. He has an accent too. "We live in White Hill, Missouri. The fella was a little eccentric, some kind of old supernatural expert. He did a few things to try to get rid of a ghost haunting little Julie and Bo, our two children. The house was clear of any trouble, for a little while. But then the ghost came back. Now it haunts us, and we don't know where to turn. Ray gave us this address. He said he wasn't sure if Alondra lived here anymore, but that if anyone could get rid of ghosts, it'd be Alondra Billington. You say Alondra's not here? Mary and I are so desperate. Where is the Hawthorne Witch now? Do you two know where we can find her?"

"I'm Cadence Wallace. I'm the Hawthorne Witch."

THE END

WITCHY ADVENTURES ARE CONTINUED IN RAVENS, BOOK 5, IN THE HAWTHORNE UNIVERSITY WITCH SERIES

THE SERIES

- BROOMSTICK
- WINDSTORM
- THE HAWTHORNE WITCH
- WITCH MIRROR
- RAVENS
- SHADOW CAST
- BELTANE FIRE short story prequel
- SAMHAIN WITCH short story (3.5)
- CANDY CRONE
- ALONDRA 20 yr prequel

THE BOXED SETS

- THE HAWTHORNE UNIVERSITY WITCH SERIES
- THE HAWTHORNE UNIVERSITY WITCH SERIES (4-6)
- THE HAWTHORNE UNIVERSITY WITCH HOLIDAY COLLECTION

AND DON'T FORGET THAT THE ENTIRE SERIES IS NOW AVAILABLE ON AUDIO, PERFORMED BY ALEXA ELMY AND PRESTON GEER!

EXCERPT FROM BOOK 5

"CHAPTER 1 - KNOCK, KNOCK, KNOCK" IN RAVENS, BOOK 5 OF THE HAWTHORNE UNIVERSITY WITCH SERIES BY A.L. HAWKE

Bryce and I are sitting together at a small wooden kitchen table enjoying a nice quiet breakfast to celebrate our anniversary. It's our second anniversary celebratory breakfast. Yeah, yesterday we had a wonderful quiet breakfast planned too, but it was interrupted by a bloody black raven with a broken wing fluttering on our porch, followed by a second knock heralding a young couple talking about their haunted house in White Hill, Missouri. Honestly, I prefer peace with my hubby. It gets my mind off all the things happening lately at Hawthorne University—like losing my soul.

I give Bryce a wink and raise my orange juice glass in a toast. The orange juice is really tart and yummy.

Then I gaze around our kitchen. I gotta tell you, my teacher, Alondra, had style. She installed Viking stoves, a marble island, and gorgeous travertine flooring. It's so lovely, like the rest of my house—or her house. Outside, through a small window, around all the thousands of trees of Hawthorne, it's a bit gloomy this morning. But it's warm and toasty indoors.

"What'cha thinking 'bout, babe?" Bryce asks, cutting sausage with a fork and knife.

"Nothing," I answer with a shrug.

There's a knock at the door—a third knock. He gets up.

"Forget it, Bryce. Let's just finish breakfast."

He nods and slowly sits back down.

"So, how was your visit with Kenosha?" He asks, forking some eggs. "You never told me. I spoke to her on the phone, but I haven't gotten to see her yet."

"I thought we weren't gonna talk about that stuff?"

"Just asking about Kenosha," he says with a shrug.

"But asking how Kenosha is doing is going to lead to talking about witchcraft. And talking about witchcraft is going to lead to discussing our coven. Talking about our coven is going to lead to your metaphysical class. And then, before you know it, professor, we're gonna talk about haunted houses, the couple yesterday, and White Hill, Missouri. And then—"

"Got it, Katie," he says with a laugh. "Forget it. So...what do we talk about then?"

"Nothing," I say with a shrug. "Absolutely nothing. That's what I really want to talk about, Bryce."

But we hear the knocking again.

"I mean, breakfast is our time to forget about our problems," I continue, ignoring the noise. I raise my orange juice glass again in a toast to him. "Happy anniversary, hun."

"Happy anniversary, babe."

But he still gets up.

He scoots his chair back and heads down our hallway. As we approach the foyer, under our crystal chandelier, something hits the door louder than ever. And it sounds a lot bigger than a bird. Bryce looks through the peep hole. He shrugs. Then he looks down.

"*Oh, my god!*"

He throws open the door.

"What is it, Bryce? Is it the bird again?"

No, it's not a small fluttering bird with a broken wing. Lying on the ground is a pale, naked woman shaking in a fetal position, bleeding from cuts all over her neck, chest, arms, and legs. There are so many cuts on her naked body that the dripping blood seems to have painted her skin red. She's weak and closing her eyes tightly. If her pretty blues opened, I'd recognize those infernal eyes. I already recognize her face: Enora. Yeah, Enora, my archenemy witch-bitch who tried to bleed me, kill my husband, turn my best friend insane, and cut Mira's throat has landed on our doorstep.

We stand over my archenemy in total shock, not doing anything. Then Bryce crouches down and lifts a blood-drenched wrist. Even her palm drips red over his hand and the sleeve of his navy blue robe. Under all that blood on her palm is the bitch's black backward pentagram.

"Bryce," Enora mutters weakly.

"Jesus, Enora, what happened to you?" I ask. But I keep my distance.

"Execrated."

"Help me take her inside, Cadence," Bryce says.

"No. No way."

"Cadence, she's hurt bad."

"So? Call 911. She can't come inside, Bryce."

"You want me to leave her by the door for dead?" he snaps, looking up. "Like the bird?"

"She probably was that bird, Bryce!"

"Come on, Cadence. Help me take her in."

"We'll just call 911, 'kay?"

"Cadence, help me bring her in," he says sternly, shaking his head.

"But why is she bleeding *everywhere*?" I ask. "There's deep red cuts and scratches all over. Was she whipped? Here's a better question, why the hell did she come here, Bryce?"

"She's wanted for murder," Bryce replies. "Kenosha threw her in jail for trying to kill Mira. Remember? She said *execrated.*

That means cursed. Maybe this was another spell by the Samhain Witch."

"Yeah, but...why did she come *here*? Does she want me to finish her off?"

"Cadence!" he says, shaking his head. "Enough. Help me bring her inside. She's not a dying bird."

"What if she dies inside the house? The cops might investigate and—"

He just looks up, still on his knee, staring right into my eyes.

"Fine. What do you want me to do?"

"Help me bring her into the guest bathroom."

He crouches down and grabs her by the shoulders. His hands slide along her skin because of all the blood. That's so gross. She's obviously unconscious. I think the slipping and sliding along her blood-drenched cuts would make her scream if she were awake. I reach down and pick up her feet. They're warm and slimy from all the fresh blood too. Then we carry her inside. I watch as all that blood drips over my lovely white marble floor.

"What are we going to do with her?" I ask.

"Clean her and dress her wounds."

"It looks like...*ew, gross!*"

"What!" he cries, backing up. Bryce nearly drops her. "What the hell is it now! What's the matter, Cadence?"

"Look at her leg, Bryce!" There's a piece of flesh dangling from her thigh surrounded by what looks like teeth marks. "I think something bit her!"

TO BE CONTINUED IN BOOK 5 OF THE HAWTHORNE
UNIVERSITY WITCH SERIES

ALSO BY A.L. HAWKE

PARANORMAL ROMANCE

- THE HAWTHORNE UNIVERSITY WITCH SERIES (I-III)
- THE HAWTHORNE UNIVERSITY WITCH SERIES (4-6)
- THE HAWTHORNE UNIVERSITY WITCH HOLIDAY COLLECTION
- SHADES
- HAUNTING JOY
- PHANTOM MASQUERADE

- MY EVIL EYE
- THE GUARDIAN
- NECTAR OF AMBROSIA
- CORA

FANTASY: THE AZURE SERIES

- HARMONIA
- CORA: RISE OF THE FALLEN GODDESS
- AZURE BLUE
- CORAL RED
- PRINCESS SOJOURN

SCIENCE FICTION

- CANDY SAVANT SERIES

Books available at https://alhawke.com/books

PARTING WORDS

What did you think of *Witch Mirror*? By placing a book review, you can inform others of your thoughts and help spread the word about my book.

Want more? Periodically I like to send news regarding current or new projects. If you'd like to be privy, I encourage you to sign up to my email newsletter. Your information will remain private and you can cancel any time.

Sign up at www.alhawke.com or scan the following QR code:

ALSO BY A.L. HAWKE

PARANORMAL ROMANCE

- THE HAWTHORNE UNIVERSITY WITCH SERIES (I-III)
- THE HAWTHORNE UNIVERSITY WITCH SERIES (4-6)
- THE HAWTHORNE UNIVERSITY WITCH HOLIDAY COLLECTION
- SHADES
- HAUNTING JOY
- PHANTOM MASQUERADE

- MY EVIL EYE
- THE GUARDIAN
- NECTAR OF AMBROSIA
- CORA

FANTASY: THE AZURE SERIES

- HARMONIA
- CORA: RISE OF THE FALLEN GODDESS
- AZURE BLUE
- CORAL RED
- PRINCESS SOJOURN

SCIENCE FICTION

- CANDY SAVANT SERIES

Books available at https://alhawke.com/books

PARTING WORDS

What did you think of *Witch Mirror*? By placing a book review, you can inform others of your thoughts and help spread the word about my book.

Want more? Periodically I like to send news regarding current or new projects. If you'd like to be privy, I encourage you to sign up to my email newsletter. Your information will remain private and you can cancel any time.

Sign up at www.alhawke.com or scan the following QR code:

ACKNOWLEDGMENTS

I want to thank my beta reader George B., my line editor Stephanie Ward, proofreader Alexa B and my cover artist Brosedesignz. This publication is so much better because of all the help from this team. Thank you!

ABOUT THE AUTHOR

A.L. Hawke is the author of the bestselling Hawthorne University Witch series. The author lives in Southern California torching the midnight candle over lovers against a backdrop of machines, nymphs, magic, spice and mayhem. A.L. Hawke writes fantasy and romance spanning four thousand years, from pre-civilization to contemporary and beyond.

Visit A.L. Hawke at www.alhawke.com

Email: contact@alhawke.com